The Parsley Parcel

Also in the Gypsy Girl trilogy

Gold and Silver Water

Freya is summoned to help Penny, a girl imprisoned in sadness. Can she find a way to unlock the healing power of gold and silver water?

Riot of Red Ribbon

Freya's greatest challenge yet. Briar Rose and Dibby Gran have mysteriously disappeared and Freya must use all her powers to find them.

The Parsley Parcel

by Elizabeth Arnold

mammoth

First published in Great Britain in 1995
by Heinemann Young Books
This TV tie-in edition published 2001
by Mammoth, an imprint of Egmont Books UK
a division of Egmont Holding Limited
239 Kensington High Street, London W8 6SA

ISBN 0 7497 4593 2

10 9 8 7 6 5 4 3 2 1

A CIP catalogue record for this title is available from the
British Library

Printed and bound in Great Britain by Cox & Wyman Ltd,
Reading, Berkshire

Contents

1   'I do not want to go!'   1
2   'My mam always has a reason!'   8
3   'Not in a million years!'   16
4   'These is wonderful happy shoes'   29
5   'My brother, my best brother'   40
6   'I am a Chime Child'   52
7   'Freya, you *must* go back!'   58
8   'Babies is awful'   78
9   'Tea on the lawn'   88
10   'Things you can't begin to understand'   97
11   'Grown-ups always cause trouble'   107
12   'Aunt Emma thought I was telling porky pies again'   119
13   'Freya, I've warned you before about not hurting people'   130
14   'You're sounding very mysterious, Freya'   137
15   'Keep your head, fulfil the drúkkerébema'   147
16   'Nobody noticed at all'   154
17   'She'll never do it, Freya!'   169
18   'Things were going very badly indeed'   181
19   'To Aunty Emma and Uncle Jack, with love from Freya'   190

For my sisters
especially D

1

'I do not want to go!'

I am Freya and my hair is black and nearly as wild as me. I am the spirit of the woodland and the salt of the earth ... or so my great-gran says, but most of all, I am me *and I do not want to go!*

'Great-gran, do you hear me? I *really* don't want to go!'

Great-gran peered down at me, from her seat high up in the vardo. Tashar, my brother, had made it for her specially, just so she could have the very best bossy-boots view. It was a small chair and it only just fitted, but from there Great-gran could rule our Romany world.

'Stop that hollering. Do you think that I have taught you all my magic for nothing, child? Now, let us be sure of something. You *will* do *exactly* as you are told.'

I stood, all silent sullen. I was happy here, close by the ancient oaks and free to play under the clear blue sky. Why should I live in a sticky brick house, like the gorgios do. Why should I?

'Go with your mother, Freya! Whoever heard of a gypsy girl being afraid to face her destiny?'

'I'm not afraid,' I lied, glaring at my great-gran.

She looked like an eagle, perched up high in her wagon like that. Her beady eyes were shiny bright and her slightly hooked nose pointed down at me. I felt as if I was about to be gobbled up for supper and very fast too, if I wasn't switched-on sensible.

'She's very young, Ostrich,' my mam said, using our wagon name for my great-grandmother. 'Can't the magic wait for another year?' my mam begged, still not at all sure about letting me go, well, not for such a very long time anyway.

I stared round our camp, avoiding my great-grandmother's penetrating gaze. Even though we moved every three days, it still always ended up looking exactly the same.

By the side of the wagons was our cooking place, with piles of wood, all neatly cut and ready to burn. Cooking pots were all laid out ready on a table. Soon, my mam would begin to prepare lunch. You can cook in a wagon, even an old one like the vardo, but we prefer not to have food smells in our beds and, anyway, outside cooking tastes full-tummy grand. Really it does.

As usual, a little pile of wood was busy burning merrily and, suspended from a special bracket, our shiny black kettle. It was almost boiling. I knew Mam would have to have a cup of tea before I had to go.

Great-gran gets quickly impatient. Mam and I had been standing root-still for far too long. So she climbed down from her favourite perch, and marched towards us. She's old as the hills, but she can still move pretty smartly when she wants to.

'This child!' she said, pointing at me as if there

2

were others, which there weren't. 'This child is a Chime Child. She is an uncommon little one, born to make the most difficult magic. Why do you think that I have spent so much time and trained her so well?'

My mam said nothing. My great-gran was sprouting words like a rusty can spills water and, when she does that, then nothing is usually the very best thing to do.

'If I remember,' my great-gran said, as if there was a shadow of doubt, 'it was *you* that suggested the magic in the first place. "Please, Ostrich," you said, "Give a drúkkerébema." *You must have known then that Freya's gifts would be needed.*'

Mam nodded. 'Yes,' she sighed and gripped my hand, 'but now the time has come . . .'

'The time is *now*. I have given a drúkkerébema,' my great-gran said, her tone implying that that was the end of the matter.

'A drúkkerébema is only a prophecy,' my mam dared to remind my great-gran, but she sounded more than a little bit desperate. 'Surely the fulfilling of the drúkkerébema can wait another year!'

'If I give a drúkkerébema, then it happens as I command,' Great-gran shouted and her voice was ear-shake loud. 'Freya was born to serve our people and *that* is *exactly* what she is going to do!'

'Can't I just take her to the house myself?' my mam pleaded. 'She's only small. Can't I just say, "Here's Freya. She's here to grant your heart's desire." '

Great-gran puffed out her chest and, just for a moment, she really did look like an ostrich. 'No,

3

you can't! Do you really think that Emma Hemmingway would believe you if you did?'

I shrugged. I think I had given up trying to stay, ages ago. 'It's OK, Mam, I'll go. Great-gran's right. She hasn't learned me all her spells for nothing.'

'But that means that I have to pretend to abandon you, Freya. No Romany woman willingly just dumps her child. We're better than them gorgios at loving children. I hate the very idea of leaving you with strangers!'

I increased my grip on my mam's hand. I held her so tight that her shiny rings bit into her olive skin and she had to pull away. 'I know you'd never just luggage-leave me without a very good reason, and you know it doesn't matter what the gorgios think.' I tried to sound really grown up. I put on my brightest smile and my most confident look. 'Great-gran has promised that I shall do some magic and so that is what I have to do.'

I glanced at the witchlike old lady that I loved so much. 'If I don't do the magic then that old choviar will eat me alive.' I was still using my grown-up voice, so that she knew that I wasn't being head-thump rude.

'And if I eats you, well, I won't even bother to spit out the pieces,' Great-gran retorted, but her eyes twinkled again, now that I was pleasing her. 'One cup of tea, Freya, and then you and your mam must leave.'

It seemed that in no time at all I was left, alone and miserable, on the busy railway platform a few miles past Strawberry Woods.

'Look lost,' my mam said, thrusting our link

4

crystal into my hand as she kissed me goodbye. 'Don't forget to look sad but try not to be deep-heart miserable. Remember, when you hold the crystal, only our bones are apart.'

She was a fine one to tell me that! She who had nagged and nagged for me to stay. It was my mam that needed the crystal joining magic. I am a Chime Child, I can cross time on my own.

'I'll remember,' I promised. 'I'll mind-think us close, but look out face-sad. Now go. Great-gran will be needing you.'

It wasn't difficult to look properly miserable. I knew I would just hate being away from home for so long. Real tears leapt out from my eyes, even though my brother Tashar was watching me from a distance, just to make sure that I was safe and things went to plan.

I *felt* like a package. I even had a label round my neck. I'd been left before, but never like this. The last time had been when my great-gran was too sick to mind me and my mam had to go and do some magic that Great-gran had already promised. That time, as usual, she was back in three days and three days is no time at all.

As I told you, I am a Chime Child. That means that I have to do extraordinary enchantments. The sort of spells that even my great-grandmother can't do. Being a Chime Child gives me special powers, and special problems too. My mam says power and problems always stick like glue, so I must be really careful. Life for me, she says, will never be sail-through easy.

I might be away from my mam for ages, weeks

possibly, and I have to get things to happen just right. My great-gran has warned me, full-head times, that if I rush too fast, then the magic will not happen.

Me and my sad face sat still for ages on that railway platform, even Tashar, my brother, kept sneaking a look at his watch.

Just as I thought that he would give up and come to collect me and take me home, a strange lady appeared and asked me my name. Now I was really scared, so scared that my tummy felt tumble-mix trembly.

I glanced across the station, to where Tashar was pretending to read a newspaper. He gave me a little nod, and when he was sure the lady couldn't see, he blew me a little kiss. Romanies are not known for being kiss-kiss minded. I knew then that I was to go with the lady and that he, too, thought I was rather small for such a big adventure.

'My name is Jane Turner,' the stiff-faced lady said. Jumpy-out tears wetted my face as I stared at the stranger. 'I'm a social worker. I'm here to help you. Somebody phoned up to say you'd just been left here. Is that right?'

Tashar nodded over his newspaper. I nodded too, and pointed at my label like my mam had shown me.

'You poor, poor mite,' the social worker said, taking my hand. 'I think that you had better come along with me.'

I was all tear-stained and finger-faced smudgy as I walked beside her on my way to my first magic. I think I must have looked more like a street waif than a magician; and hopefully that was just as it should be.

2

'My mam always has a reason!'

I didn't intend to look sullen, but there they were, the grown-ups, talking over my head as if I was stupid or something.

'She might prove difficult!' Jane Turner was trying to talk quietly, but I was quite sure that the whole street could hear. I shifted my feet and my face went bright red with embarrassment. It wasn't my fault that I had a social worker after all, especially one with such huge, foghorn-mouth whispers.

'It's happened before, Mrs Hemmingway. Her mother just ups and disappears.' She was whispering now, and I knew that I shouldn't have heard, but I have very sharp ears. I couldn't stand hearing any more. I stopped wishing the world would swallow me up, and started feeling really angry.

'My mam always has a reason!' I shouted. 'My mam would *never* just up and leave me.' I stood as tall as I could, my black eyes boring into her faded blue ones as I tried to shock her into silence. I failed or maybe her eyelids were too heavy, so heavy she couldn't feel the malice in my stare.

'But she did, Freya,' the social worker insisted,

in that I'm-going-to-keep-calm-even-though-I-want-to-kill-you voice that adults have. 'She left you like a parcel. You even had a cardboard label. I'm sorry, darling, but that is the truth.'

I felt tears filling my eyes. It wasn't fair! My mam was lovely. She'd *never* just leave me, *never*. Whenever my mam did something, there was always a reason. Anyway, I knew there was a *proper* purpose. I was, after all, here to fulfil the drúkkerébema. It was just that I wasn't allowed to tell. I'd had to promise to bite my tongue, no matter how much they poky-pried, and twisted my tummy with crossness.

'How exciting! Were you really left like a parcel?' Mrs Hemmingway asked, trying to distract me.

I shook my head. 'I had a label because my mam said it was important. She wanted to be sure that exactly the right things happened.'

'See!' the social worker said, her face all gleeful. 'See, she admits it herself. The label even had your name and address on it.'

'Perhaps her mother does have a good reason,' the lady called Mrs Hemmingway replied gently. 'It's possible that she's heard about me from her friends. I have had little travellers to care for before, after all.'

I smiled with relief. Perhaps things wouldn't be *so* bad. I sniffed back my tears and offered Mrs Hemmingway a big bright smile. 'I'm not a traveller. Them's modern things. I'm a Romany . . . and proud of it.'

'She's a didakai,' the social worker explained. She meant no harm but she was wrong.

I scowled and gave the social worker my best evil look. 'I'm a Romany. There's no impure blood in me. I'm one of the last proper gypsies. That's what I am. I'm not a tinker, or a poshrat. Nor am I a mucky modern traveller. I am a *proper* Romany gypsy. I know more about some things than you outside folk will ever learn, not in all your life-living days.'

'If you want to be called a gypsy then that's fine by me,' Mrs Hemmingway said quietly. 'We were trying to protect you. It's just that some people use the word to be rude.'

'Then them's too daft to understand!' I said firmly.

'Well, in this case, I would imagine that you know what's best.' Mrs Hemmingway gave me a reassuring smile. I could tell that it was from-the-heart real. I smiled back, just to show I was grateful.

'See? She's a changeling child, a moody moppet with strangely adult ways,' the social worker confided. Mrs Hemmingway nodded in agreement, but when the social worker looked away she winked at me.

'I've fostered loads of children,' Mrs Hemming-way said. 'I don't suppose Freya will prove any more difficult than the rest.' She offered the social worker a bright competent smile that meant 'now-go-away' and, suddenly, I knew that Jane Turner annoyed her as well. I felt a little happier. I tried to remember what my mam had said about not missing her and about learning from experience. It was going to be difficult. Already I yearned for wide open fields and Romany tents and caravans. Already I missed my mam.

Mrs Hemmingway led me into her bright shiny house, with not a thing out of place, and offered me tea. There was beefburger, chips and ice-cream, my favourite. Suddenly I was famished. I ate up in seconds.

I don't think Mrs Hemmingway was very impressed with my manners. I saw her eyebrows rise when I forgot to close my mouth properly, and when I got hiccups because I drank my tea too fast. I didn't say sorry. Why should I? She was the one who was mad enough to want to share her posh house with a Romany child like me.

I was very tired. I'd hung about in offices and corridors for ages while people planned my future. Mrs Hemmingway must've guessed. I was allowed to have a lovely deep bath, all by myself.

'It will relax you, darling,' Mrs Hemmingway told me, as she checked I had enough fluffy towels and things. She even gave me her blue smelly bottle, but she warned me not to use too much.

I tipped out all the stuff in the bottle. Soap bubbles blew up like mad; overflowing the bath and cascading down to the floor. It was such fun. I swirled about and nearly drowned in a mountain of bubble-blue mist. Desperate not to cause *too* much trouble, I tried to stuff some of the bubbles back, but they frothed up even more. I wondered if Aunt Emma would laugh or cry, to see such a mess on her squeaky clean floor.

11

My body smelled posh and my skin was all red and crinkly from soaking so much. That's one thing that we Romanies don't get much chance to do, soak. I had to be really careful, climbing out of that bubble-slippy bath.

Mrs Hemmingway never said a word. She just told me she liked to be called Aunt Emma and gave me a nearly new nightie with pretty bows to wear. She said she always kept one in the house, just in case, whatever that meant.

Within minutes of being popped into bed I was fast asleep. That's not like me. I never normally sleep, not until I'm sure that I've missed nothing interesting. I am poky-nose curious, just like my great-gran.

I woke up bright and early next morning, just like I usually do, and decided it was time to explore. Aunt Emma, and her husband . . . who I was instructed to call Uncle Jack, were still sand-man sleeping. I crept down the stairs, stood on a stool, and stretched up high in order to reach the top lock, to go out into the back garden.

I love early mornings, especially the ones that are dressed in a bridal gown of frost, mixed with the crispy promise of a real spring day to follow. The air that day smelled fresh-grass sweet, even though there was not a green bit to be seen. It wasn't bad at all for an estate place, though not nearly as good as the rich scent of open fields, close to deep pine woods.

The garden was bigger than I expected. It was all neat and tidy like the house. There wasn't a bit of wild. I love natural things, places where there's bees and butterflies, clover and lady's slipper to be found. Here, there were regulation rows of neat plants, none of which had a name I knew and my mam says that I'm very good at knowing what plants are called. The flowers in this garden were all neatly laid out, like soldiers on parade. They stood to attention round a boringly perfect lawn, in exact little patterns. I wondered if they took them away if they didn't grow to their proper size.

I imagined Aunt Emma and Uncle Jack out on their hands and knees on Sunday, but they weren't praying, oh no! They were carefully measuring every blade of grass and trimming it back with scissors if it should dare to grow too tall. I had to laugh out loud. What hours they must waste, trying to make a garden look like a wall-hung picture.

My stomach began to be hungry. Back home we had breakfast when the sun came up, and it had long since risen. My great-gran, who is as old as old, reckons that days are too short to waste sleeping.

I was about to go back inside when I spotted a little path with tiny stone steps, leading through some nearly closed bushes. I followed the path down, being careful not to slip. I was now in the colder part of the garden where Jack Frost had been even more overnight busy. He had given everything really big crystal kisses, that glittered like jewels in the morning light.

It was magic! A really secret, secret garden! It was a proper garden, all growing spread-wild natural. There was willow and nettles and lots of lovely grasses, like cocksfoot, catstail and rye. There was celandine and primrose. The primroses were the right sort, which is soft butter yellow, not those bright gaudy ones that the gorgios like so much. There were frogs, all croaking as loud as they could, because it was time to make frog's-spawn jelly eggs. It was lovely.

'Hello, little one, did you sleep well?'

Emma Hemmingway had crept up so quietly, and I had been so absorbed in the morning, that I hadn't heard her, even though I have what my mam calls hear-too-much-for-my-own-good ears.

'Freya, good morning, did you sleep well?'

I nodded. 'Fancy you having a *proper* garden.'

'Well, it does make for lovely butterflies and I do like to feel that I'm doing a little for conservation. I'm also glad that you're not making a noise, Freya, especially so early on Sunday morning.'

'Why?'

'Well, the new vicar and his wife live the other side of the hedge. Mrs Plumpton is, I'm told, a little set in her ways. She thinks children should be seen and not heard. All that old-fashioned stuff.'

'Oh, like you!'

I had to give her credit. Mrs Hemmingway, Aunt Emma that is, laughed. 'Worse than me,' she said.

'I can't see no church. I can't even see a spire.'

'Mrs Plumpton lives in the vicarage, not in the church, Freya. The church is at the bottom of the garden next door.'

I stood up, as tall as I could. 'I still can't see a church, or a spire.'

14

'It's behind those yews. It's quite pretty. On Sundays you can come to church with us, if you like.'

'Me and my bubble-burst mouth!' I groaned, as I walked back up to the house with Aunt Emma. I swear she grinned at my hot-head crossness. I think she thought it funny, me having to attend a big long service, and get bang-head bored.

'Churches is for gorgio weddings,' I told Aunt Emma crossly, 'and all-folk funerals, not for praying until it's a fair time to die.'

'Nonsense. A church service can be a wonderful thing. Uncle Jack and I go to church quite often and you can come too.'

I didn't say anything. I didn't want to trouble-tease too early ... well, not before breakfast anyway. I ate my buttered toast in silence. Not because it was lovely buttery hot, but because I was thinking.

This magic was going to be much more difficult to make than I had thought. Aunt Emma wasn't supposed to like me too much at first. She had to decide to help a child in need, not a child she was overmuch fond of. The gift that I was going to give her required a sacrifice. First of all, she had to do something that she really didn't want to do and she had to do it for *me*.

15

3

'Not in a million years!'

'Come on, let's go shopping,' Mrs Hemmingway said the following morning when Uncle Jack had gone to work and I had paced about her great big house so much that I made her feel quite nervous. 'You need some trainers for school.'

'My mam is muddle-minded over whether I shall go to school. She says that I learns more being with her and too much schooling makes Romanies soggy-brain simple. My mam says school fills your mind with all useless facts and then you remember nothing important, like how to survive on your wits.'

'But you are required to go to school, aren't you?'

'Not by my mam, I ain't.'

'Well, I think you could do with some shoes anyway . . . just in case.'

I don't like shops and I don't need shoes. Most of all I don't need charity. 'These sandals will do me kushti!'

I glared at Mrs Hemmingway, even though I knew that she was trying to be kind. 'My mam

16

will be back soon. She'll not want to see me in big heavy shoes that are bend-toe bad for my feet.'

Mrs Hemmingway's hands tightened as she strove to control the wave of irritation threatening to overwhelm her. Just for a moment I felt sorry for being so awkward. She looked really tired of trying to be nice to me.

'My mam says nobody gets something for nothing, nobody. And my great-gran says to make a spell work, you have to pay, either in money or love.' I bit my tongue. I wished I'd not tongue-tumbled out about spells but, to my relief, Aunt Emma seemed not to have noticed.

I was quite enjoying the chance to be awkward. I hate shopping. It's not fun-filled for me, not with all those people sardine-packed and rushing out to buy not-needed packages.

Buy just the things that you need and then ponder-potter walk, that's what I think. *Much* better for you. My mam tells me that, all the time. She says staying in houses, even wagons, is just a waste of fresh-air living.

'I hate shopping. I want to stay here.'

Usually I would get tongue-lashed ears when I'm pig-head stubborn, but I was sure that *nice* Mrs Hemmingway would give in.

'I'll stay home. You go and shop by yourself. I'll even get supper ready for Uncle Jack. I can cook. My mam taught me all proper. Cooking is easy. We Romany chavis learn to cook when your gorgio girlies are still teddy-bear tied.'

'Freya, I don't doubt your culinary brilliance,

17

but you *really* do need decent shoes. Those sandals are almost worn away.'

'My mam says shoes is . . . restrictive. Clumpy shoes stop toes growing proper. My mam says real leather sandals are best. My big brother Tashar made these for me specially. My prala Tashar is real hot stuff with leather.'

Mrs Hemmingway tried to hang grimly on to her patience. Stone the crows, she was thinking impatiently, will this child never do *anything* without an argument?

'Why do you want to stone crows? It's stupid!'

I'd mind-read without even thinking. The words had leapt into my head, clear as day. My mam and I often thought-talked, but she had said never, ever to do it with strangers, even if I felt a little lonely because our bones were fair-miles parted.

'What did you say?'

Aunt Emma's face was a picture! I had to laugh, even though I'd been full fluffy feather-brained to answer her thinking words.

'Stoning crows is stupid!' I continued, despite wishing that I had buttoned my lip real tight. I was, however, rather pleased to see her so shaken. She, who knew everything, and nothing about good-for-feet shoes.

'My mam says farmers who shoot crows and hang them on fences are stupid. My mam says that crows are clever and should be respected, as they tells you things.'

'Clever crows or not, we still have to go shopping,' Aunt Emma retorted, looking a hint shaky, I thought. 'I could buy you trainers. Lots of children will be wearing them. What did you run in before?'

'Bare feet. My mam says bare feet is strong feet. If ever I want feet clothes, then Tashar makes them for me. Mostly I wear my feet nude, so that they can properly breathe.'

'Well, you can't at school! At school, bare feet are cut feet. I assume you'll go some time?'

I shook my head. The very idea made me feel a little scared. I am a free spirit. My mam had told me so and so had my great-gran. They had taught me everything that I needed to know.

I wanted the drúkkerébema to be done. I wanted my mam to come back. I did not fancy being trapped in a shanty-town school.

We walked hand in hand, even though I promised not to run away. Aunt Emma was silent, trying to make a list in her head of the things she meant to do. She was puzzled too, wondering how I had known that she was thinking of crows.

Grown-ups are funny like that. Nearly all children can mind-read. If they want to, that is. They learn while they are in their mother's tummy. Even when they are still far unborn, they can understand things. That's how a baby tells who its mam is: by thoughts, smells, sounds and everything.

Adults forget that, as you grow taller, your instinct mind closes. My mam says it always happens, unless you learn in fresh air like me, with folks who aren't scared because you know what they're thinking.

I was lucky that day! We never did get to finish

19

shopping. There we were, bustling along the street ... well, Aunt Emma was bustling. I was dragging my feet, even though they were nice and comfy in my well-worn sandals. I was dragging my feet because I was bored. Dead bored. I was trying to pull Aunt Emma backwards, even though she had tight hold of my hand, and was pulling me on. It was like we were playing seesaw on legs.

Everything changed when we reached Town Bridge and I spotted it. 'Look!'

'What?' Aunt Emma didn't even glance, and her voice was fair irritable.

'That horrid cat's got a poor little baby bird!'

Aunt Emma made the mistake of letting go of my hand, as she spotted the large ginger tom dragging its victim into the straggly bushes on the side of the bank.

'We have to save it,' I yelled, and I chased after the big old cat, that was too fat to run very fast anyway.

'It's nature!' Aunt Emma called, desperate to get me back clean and tidy. 'It's nature! I should have thought that *you*, of all people, would have known that.'

I did! That was the point. I knew full well that I shouldn't have interfered, but it was a silly old tom-cat anyway, home-fed fat, it was. It didn't ought to have a little chíriko to tease to death. Anyway, I wanted an excuse to take a little bit of nature back to Aunt Emma's polish-posh house. I wanted a friend who understood me.

I dived into the scratchy old bushes on the side of Town Bridge and yanked hold of the tail of the silly old cat. It was fair cross and hissed and spat. I took no notice! My name is Freya Boswell. We Boswells are feared of nothing, especially stupid old tom-cats that are a hissy bit cross when you steal their dinner.

'Careful, Freya!'

I ignored Mrs Hemmingway, who thought she was Aunt Emma, even though she stood frantically waving her arms at me. I knew she wanted to scream in anger, but didn't dare. She, who was ever so nice, from the tip of her neatly curled head to the end of her highly polished shoes.

I ignored, too, the cross old tom-cat and his dirty scratchy claws that drew blood even more efficiently than the thorn-spiked bushes. Finally, I ignored the pain and the noise and everything except the bird.

In a moment the fight was over. I was Boswell victorious. In my hand I held a tiny near-naked feather baby. It did have pin-pricks of feathers showing, but little else, other than chicken-plucked skin. It stared at me with scaredy eyes and I held it ever so carefully, so as not to hurt it.

'Look at the state of you!'

I didn't apologise. Why should I?

'It's natural to rescue things, isn't it?' I said, looking lip-drop resentful. 'You should be really proud that I saved something. I think that I was lion-heart brave.'

Aunt Emma looked as if she was about to blow a fuse. She stared down at me, and her face was dressed in crosspatch blotches.

'Put that dirty thing down at once! Uncle Jack will go mad if you bring that thing home.'

'No!' I didn't care what Uncle Jack thought, not a bit.

'Put that bird back in the bushes, where its mother will find it.'

'You know nothing! Its mother won't come back, not with it smelling of tom-cat and people. She'll never find it anyhow. That stupid old ginger tom could've dragged it miles before we appeared.'

'Freya *please* put it down. Let's go home and clean you up. You look as if you've been dragged through a hedge backwards.'

I stared at her in disbelief. Grown-ups can be so stupid at times. 'Well, I have, haven't I.'

'Come home! We can't possibly go shopping with your hands and face all scratched and dirty.'

'I won't come home. Not unless the chíriko fledgeling can come too.' I gave Aunt Emma my best defiant look. 'I mean it. If I can't have the bird, then I shall run away.'

Aunt Emma ignored that threat. Somehow she knew that I didn't mean it. Somehow she guessed that I *had* to stay.

'Freya, we are going home this minute. Now put down that bird at once!' Nice Aunt Emma was getting to be very stamp-foot cross indeed.

'No, it will only die. How can you think of letting it die?'

'Freya, it will only die anyway. You can't possibly look after it.'

'Yes, us can! We can care for it properly well.'

22

Aunt Emma didn't even notice that I'd used the word *us* to show that she could help too.

'Freya!'

Freya, Freya, Freya! all the time. Freya, do this, Freya, do that. Why couldn't I get my way sometimes too? I wasn't just acting difficult now. I really wanted to keep the chíriko baby.

'Don't you CARE about babies? How come, if you like children, you got stuck with me? Is the truth that only bigger people really suit you? Won't anybody let you have a proper baby to look after?'

Aunt Emma's face went white as a sheet as I attacked her. I knew instantly that I'd hit her weak spot dead centre. I changed tack. My mam says never use more force than is needed, kindness is better, and people are much the same as hosses. A light rein leads further in the long run.

'Please, Aunt Emma . . . pretty please,' I hung my head and dressed it all pathetic, 'and I'm sorry if I upset you, it's just that I really would like to try and save this poor little bird.'

'Well, *you'll* have to look after it,' Aunt Emma said, suddenly past-fighting tired. 'Remember that, Freya Boswell. *You* do the looking after.'

'Oh yes, Aunt Emma. I promise.'

'It will probably die anyway,' Aunt Emma said, more to herself than me. 'I expect it will be stiff as a board by morning.'

That didn't help. It just made me all the more determined that the little chíriko should live. I was lucky that the silly old tom-cat had been too old and too senile to do much more than scare the little bird half out of its newly feathering skin.

Aunt Emma might be the grown-up, but I was going to prove her very wrong indeed.

I kept up with Aunt Emma as she marched me home. I had the baby bird in my hand, and my hand tucked carefully under my coat. I waited for Aunt Emma to tell me that the bird would surely mess up my clothes, but she didn't bother. She probably thought they were too scruffy to worry about anyway. I wouldn't mind betting she intended to change my coat as she changed everything else.

I tried to imagine her with sicky babies and dirty nappies, but I couldn't. I thought of Pansy, my baby sister, and how my mam had sat up all night with her. I couldn't see Aunt Emma doing that.

It seemed ages until we got home. I rushed inside as soon as Aunt Emma had opened the big wooden door.

'Can you hold the bird, please?'

'Who, me?' Aunt Emma seemed shocked at the very idea of letting the tiny scrap of creature touch her very clean hands.

'Please . . . I need you.' The words stuck in my throat but I said them anyway.

Reluctantly, Aunt Emma opened her hand and allowed me to place in her care the almost lifeless bird.

'If you wrap your other hand over the top, it will keep him warm.'

Aunt Emma did as she was told. She stood in the middle of her nice clean kitchen as if I was the grown-up and she was the child. I climbed up to the top cupboard where the sweet things were kept and helped myself to honey. Aunt Emma said not a word. She stood rooted to the spot, her hands neatly folded as if she was clutching a purse and not a nearly dead bird. I carefully put a teaspoon full of honey into a cup and added hot water. When it was dissolved, I added cold water too, so it shouldn't be too hot to drink. Aunt Emma just watched. She didn't say a word.

'I need a dropper or a straw.'

Aunt Emma stopped being shocked and started getting helpful. 'I might be able to find a dropper. Uncle Jack had some eardrops last month. He had a really bad ear infection, you know. He had to have nearly a week off work and that's not like him at all, his work means everything to him. Could you make use of that dropper? I didn't throw out his medicine, just in case. Would it help?'

I nodded. Aunt Emma handed me back the fledgeling and went hunting for the dropper. She took ages washing and rinsing it clean, but eventually she handed it over and just stood watching.

I held the little chíriko in my left hand and sang softly to show it that I was its friend. It lay as calm as you like and just watched me. It and Aunt Emma . . . both of them.

'Why honey?'

'It's best.'

'I thought sugar was good for shock.'

'My great-gran says honey is better on the stomach. She says the young and the old should be pampered. Them what is not as tough as old boots should have only the best. She learned me a song:

> *Honey for the young,*
> *Honey for the old,*
> *Honey for them what is*
> *Stuffed up with cold.'*

Aunt Emma snorted, but I ignored her. She'd be proved wrong, she would. I'd make this small creature live. I'd show her!

I filled the dropper with honeyed water and put a drop on the side of the baby bird's beak. It spluttered and swallowed. I gave Aunt Emma a smile, to show her that that was what should happen, and to my surprise she seemed pleased and smiled back.

I offered my baby bird another couple of drops and then wrapped it carefully in my softest T-shirt.

'Perhaps we should buy you a new T-shirt too, next time we go shopping.'

I nodded, just to keep her happy. I really didn't care. The baby bird closed its eyes and went to sleep.

'What now?' Aunt Emma asked.

'We must make it a nest.'

'Oh!' Aunt Emma said, in the tone that meant she wished that she had never asked. We eyed one another like unmet stallions.

'Straw?'

'Not in this house!'

I pouted. Aunt Emma sighed. We glared at one another.

'How about a cardboard box stuffed with newspaper?'

That seemed to make sense. 'My dibby gran is one for sleeping on newspaper. I used to worry, but my mam says it doesn't hurt her and it keeps her warm. She can't help being stupidly scared of nice fluffy blankets.'

'Why is she scared of blankets?'

'She's scared of lots of things. She got hit on the head by a wooden wheel hub when she was small. The family were helping to harvest. Someone moved the haycart, not ever guessing that she was there.'

'That's sad, Freya.'

'Not really . . . she seems happy enough. No worries like us, that's what my mam says.'

Aunt Emma shredded the newspaper with the small print, that she took so long to read at breakfast time.

'Is that why your mam and your great-gran are so close?'

'I suppose, but mostly it's just because we're family.'

I carefully lifted the baby bird off my T-shirt and placed it in the newspaper bed. We put lots in, so that it could snuggle down and keep real warm. Only its beak and its beady eyes showed.

'Has it had enough to eat?' Aunt Emma asked.

'I need to feed it every hour.'

'Through the night?' Aunt Emma raised her eyebrows. 'Well, you'll be a quiet bunny tomorrow then,' she said, as she went to prepare tea.

I pretended not to notice the look in her eye.

The look that said: 'You'll never do that! Not in a million years! Not waking up every hour.'

4

'These is wonderful happy shoes'

I was heavy-lid tired. I'd worried myself for ages overnight, trying to plan how I would carry my chíriko about with me. She was pin-prick-feather naked, and, because she needed feeding so often until she was safe-size bigger, I wouldn't be able to leave her anywhere. Well, not for more than an hour or so, anyway.

Every time she squeaked in the night, I scrambled out of bed to give her watered-down milk, mixed with a hint of honey. All the time, I fretted about what I was going to do in the morning.

As the clock struck three, it came to me. I would have to convert my lovely red-tasselled carry bag into a baby-bird home.

Every time the chíriko woke me up, I organised a little more. First, I ferreted through the wardrobe and found a white shoe box. I used this to make a firm base in my bag. That way the sides couldn't cave in. I was frightened that if the sides folded, all soft, over my bird's tiny beak it could stop its feather-baby breathing. That was the hard bit done. After that, I felt like I could sleep a little easier.

The next time that I had to get up, I raided the bathroom. I padded my shoe box with cotton-wool balls. These, I decided, would keep my fledgeling warm and be easy to change, if they became too dirty. I only put in enough to keep the bottom clean and make a bit of snuggle room. I tore them all up to marble size, just in case they could be dangerous too. It took me ages.

Finally, I found as many soft tissues as I could, some from the spare bedroom, some from the bathroom and even some from the kitchen. I packed them into the little pocket on the side of the carry bag. I was quite sure that they'd prove very useful indeed. If I changed things every day, then maybe my lovely carry bag would smell clean and sweet, even if it was stuffed full of snuggled-up bird.

In the morning, I was sleep-needing sluggish. Somehow, I just couldn't get on at all. Aunt Emma took to looking at her watch and telling me that, if I wouldn't dust, then I was to be quiet so that she could.

She was torn between completing her endless housework and buying me the trainers that meant she could throw my nice old sandals into the bin, as soon as she thought that I'd forgotten about them, that is. She hadn't a hissing hope! Not when Tashar had embossed them with flowers especially for me.

I felt too tired to work and was soon bored with being good inside. I asked if I could play in the garden. Aunt Emma stopped clock watching and duster waving. She made up her mind.

'Well, you mustn't get dirty, Freya. I think that we should do the shopping first, after all.'

I didn't argue. At least I would get the chance to test out my carry bag home. If I behaved well and Aunt Emma was busy, we might successfully complete the shopping in record time. The one thing about being house-proud, I guess, is that if you think it's dusty at home, then shopping becomes less attractive. That was fine by me. I'd rather gather herbs with my mam, and learn how to make concoctions. It's just like cooking really, but much more fun. Maybe, if I asked nicely, Aunt Emma would let me plant some things in her garden. My mam and I plant little secret gardens everywhere. That way, there are always fresh herbs to be harvested, no matter where we are living.

'If we *must* go shopping, then I like seeds and things. Can we buy them too, please,' I said, minding my best manners in order to please her. If I could have my own little garden, then I could more easily mind-call my mam. She would know exactly where to find me, up to my ears in green, as usual.

Aunt Emma gave me a long hard look. The sort that told me that, so far, I hadn't a hope. I hadn't impressed her much. In fact, I hadn't impressed her at all!

'I like to play the piano and read books, but we all have to do the less amusing things, like helping with housework and shopping for trainers.'

'Gypsies don't need shoes,' I reminded Aunt Emma, hoping at least to make the shopping time pass faster.

'Freya, while you're with me, you'll wear shoes.

31

I suggest that we make a simple agreement. *You* accept a pair of shoes with good grace and *I'll* accept sharing part of my house with a small, but very smelly bird.'

Satisfied that she had made her point, Aunt Emma gave me a smile that was a lot more friendly than her looks before. 'Anyway, I thought you were called travellers now.'

'Travellers is anybody who travels. Tinkers, didakai, mumpers, anybody. I am a proper gypsy, a Romany. My tribe goes way back to the Athinganoi. That's what my great-gran says, anyway.'

'And is your great-gran to be believed?'

'Of course she is! Though my mam says I should take her life tales with just a *pinch* of salt.'

'I think your mam sounds very wise.' Aunt Emma brushed an imaginary hair off my coat. 'So you don't mind being called a gypsy then?'

I held my head proud-hoss high. 'No, I like being a gypsy . . . a proper one. My mam says I am what I am and that's all right!'

'Perfectly correct! But I am what I am, too. So we'll keep to our agreement and go and get shoes right now.'

Even though I wanted the shopping to be over really fast, I nagged. I can't help it, it's my nature. Anyway, by now I'd discovered that I quite enjoyed annoying Aunt Emma, even though she was really nice, and, even better than that, I had an excuse. The drúkkerébema demanded she work for her heart's desire. I tugged her hand, and tried for the seeds once more.

'Why can't we gather seeds? Seeds like parsley.'

'Parsley? Freya, I don't think there's time today . . . and why parsley?'

I gave Aunt Emma what my great-gran describes as my knowing look. 'Those who don't like gypsies say only the wild-ways wicked grow parsley. I suppose *you* think *I'm* too wicked.' I decided to finish by winding her up good and proper. 'Let me grow parsley, Aunt Em. It will be fun . . . really evil!'

'Well, I expect you can be pretty evil,' Aunt Emma said and I'm sure she was smothering a smile as she spoke, 'most children can. Perhaps I'll let you grow parsley . . . another day. A day when you're not so wicked that you refuse to help, even just a little, in the house.'

I was shocked. I was NOT wicked. I stamped my feet in rage and gave Aunt Emma my best pout. Nobody had ever called me wicked before.

Aunt Emma realised she had made a big mistake. She stared into my eyes which were dark pools of black anger. 'Freya, I was only teasing!'

'You wasn't!'

'I was, Freya. Honestly. Why, if it was wicked and evil to grow parsley, then how come the vicar has so much of it in his garden?'

'Can we get some seeds then?' I asked, never slow to take advantage.

'Not today. Today we are far too busy. As I said, you *will* have new shoes.'

I tried not to sulk. My mam says, if the wind changes, you stay poky-lip stuck-faced for ever.

The shoe shop was big and crowded and I hated it. The shop assistants all wore neat black dresses with lots of buttons and piping. They stood clumped together in a corner, trying to pretend that everybody was so busy looking at shoes that they didn't want any help at all.

Aunt Emma coughed politely, but the shop girls kept on talking about their silly boyfriends and what they had done last night. Aunt Emma coughed again, this time just a little bit louder. One of the other shoe-buying ladies gave Aunt Emma a smile, one that showed that she thought the girls were very rude too, being so slow to serve them.

I got fed up. I pulled my hand out of Aunt Emma's and marched up to the mouthy shop girl, who made my great-gran seem quiet as quiet, when she never, ever was.

'My Aunt Emma insists on buyin' me shoes.'

'What shoes?'

'Trainers.'

The shop girl pointed to the far corner where there were hundreds of trainers all in long racks. I glanced at Aunt Emma who had a strange look on her face and was pretending not to have noticed that I had gone.

'My Aunt Emma says that my feet are to be measured and that someone in this shop will make sure it's done proper!'

The shop girl stared at me. I glared back at her, letting my black eyes bore deep into her skull. She shifted uneasily. 'OK, sunshine, you win. Let's get you measured *proper*.'

I ignored her sarcasm and Aunt Emma's deep rich chuckle. I stomped over to the machine and allowed my feet to be measured in every direction that you could think of.

'Size 2F,' the shop girl said after a while. 'That's quite big feet for a little person like you . . . even if you do have a mouth to match.'

'My mam says if you doesn't ask you doesn't get! My Aunt Emma is a busy lady, with lots of dusting to do, so if you would KINDLY go to the trouble of bringing us size 2F-type trainers, and then we'll not mind you talking about your silly boyfriend while we try them on!'

Aunt Emma sidled up to me as the shop assistant rushed off, with her face dressed red and cross, to fetch boxes. 'That was more than a little bit rude, Freya!'

'Good though, wasn't it? I heard you laugh.'

'What, me, Freya? I don't *think* so.'

'You're twisty-tongue teasing again, aren't you?'

'Well, maybe . . . just a little.'

I took off my carry bag and propped it carefully up against the side of a shiny black chair. 'If I must have shoe clothes,' I told Aunt Emma, 'then at least I can make the buying fun.'

We tried on lots of shoes. Not because I needed to, I'd seen the best ones straight away. No, we tried on lots of shoes because we both knew that the shop lady who was too busy talking to serve would have to clear them all up again afterwards.

I left the tried-on ones all muddled and Aunt Emma forgot to remind me to be tidy. In fact she was so busy helping me choose, that she didn't seem to notice the mess at all. When I was really fed up with size 2F I tried on the last pair of all.

The ones that I had known that I wanted, right at the very start.

'Can I have these, please, Aunt Emma?'

'Do you really like them, Freya? Don't you think they're just a little bit bright perhaps?' Aunt Emma asked, obviously convinced that by tomorrow I'd refuse to be seen dead in them.

I could see what she meant. Mostly, the trainers were white, with discreet little patterns. These were bright and stripy and such beautifully happy shoes.

'My mam says that life is dull enough. Always go for something bright, my mam says, it adds a little colour to living. Anyway, I'll only wear them at your house.'

Aunt Emma didn't argue. She just paid up and smiled a happy smile, as she let me carry the bright plastic bag. Today, shopping had been fun. Today had been a really nice change. I reached up and kissed her on the cheek. Just so that she should know that I wasn't always rude.

As we'd been so long shopping, we had to stop so that I could feed my little bird. We sat close together on a wooden bench, in the handkerchief-sized town park. Aunt Emma held the shopping, while I dropped honey water and milk on to the tiny fledgeling's beak.

'It's amazing nobody noticed the bird,' Aunt Emma said, 'nearly as amazing as you getting up to feed it every hour. Uncle Jack and I never really believed that you'd manage to do that.'

'It's the reason why I didn't want to dust! I'd done all *my* work, when you were slump-head sleeping.'

36

Chíriko bird stared bright-eyed from his cotton-wool bed, deep in my carry bag, then he squawked for a few seconds.

'His feathers are growing through more. Soon I shall know what he is,' I told Aunt Emma.

'He's certainly very hungry today. I'm glad he was quiet in that shop. One squawking person was quite enough for that shop assistant to handle. Imagine how cross she'd have been to have two!'

'You're teasing again, aren't you?' I said, wiping off the spilt stuff from the baby bird's face, in an effort to stop him smelling so much. 'He needs some proper food . . . like worms and things.'

'I think he might still be too small,' Aunt Emma advised. 'His parents would be giving him regurgitated food still.'

'What's that?'

'Food that's been chomped up like a stew.'

'My dibby gran makes a good stew.'

'Even if I made you a stew, it would be rather a lot for one small bird. I mean, you wouldn't want to eat it too, would you? Not if it wasn't as good as the one made by your dibby gran.'

I sighed and, so as not to upset her, I said, 'I 'spect your stew isn't too bad,' after all, how could I carry on being so nasty, when she had been so nice. 'But if the stew is too much, what shall we use? How shall we full-tummy fill the baby bird?'

'What if I bought a pot of baby-food stew, lots of meat and vegetables all mashed up with vitamins and minerals. Shall we try that?'

I packed my chíriko baby up carefully and settled him back in his bag. He went straight to

37

sleep, in the nice safe, dark place that had taken me so long to make. We had to go into yet another shop to buy baby food in a jar, but it was worth it. We looked all along the shelf and decided that stew was best, because we weren't sure yet what sort of bird we had. Aunt Emma bought two jars and two ice-creams.

I put my carry bag over my shoulder and held my bright plastic shoe bag in one hand and a huge cornet with chocolate in it in the other.

'We shouldn't really eat in the street,' Aunt Emma told me, 'but just this once it will do no harm.'

She was doing it again! She was being really nice. I felt properly guilty, about being so nicky-picky-tongued. By now I was almost convinced that she would be nice to anybody. Even the most horrid child in the world. As my great-gran says, there is none so strange as folk.

I bit into my ice-cream, pretending not to notice the frothy moustache that appeared because I was greedy-mouthed. I slurped again. This time I got a blob on my nose too. I half lifted my face, expecting it to be wet-hanky scrubbed. Aunt Emma took no notice! She pretended my face was fresh-spring sparkley. Perhaps she just doesn't think much to licking face-scrub hankies. I wiped my face on my sleeve, and loaded myself up with bags.

We walked home in carefree mood. I'd chosen red and yellow trainers.

'They're favourite gypsy colours,' I explained.

'Why?'

'Because, well, because they are. Happy colours

38

are in our blood and these shoes have bright pink heel flashes, pink as those primrose things that you can buy in flower shops, when the proper ones should be soft golden yellow. These is wonderful happy shoes, Aunt Emma!'

Aunt Emma smiled. 'Well, Freya, I have to admit that it was really good fun buying them. Such fun that I think I should always take you shopping.'

I scowled. I got ready to be touchy-tongued, but then I realised that she was only teasing. I switched on my best sunshine smile. The really happy smile that lights up your eyes. I took Aunt Emma's hand without being asked and let her lead me home.

If I was cross-heart honest, I was pleased. If I had to have shoes then they were the best. I couldn't wait to show them to Uncle Jack. I hoped that he wouldn't be too late home. Uncle Jack was worse than my great-gran in thinking that every hour should be busy-bee filled.

5

'My brother, my best brother'

I wasn't going to let Aunt Emma bin my sandals. 'I *have* to keep them,' I told her firmly.

'Why? Surely you can see how dangerous they are?'

'They'll last for ages yet. These are *properly* made, using real long-life leather that my prala Tashar had specially cured. The leather is properly soft and embossed with tiny daisy flowers. How on earth can you even think that I will throw them away?'

Uncle Jack looked at me from over his newspaper. 'Who's Tashar?'

'My brother, my best brother. Sometimes he lets me work with him, sometimes he even *asks* me to come.'

Uncle Jack lowered his newspaper and folded it neatly. Aunt Emma gave him another cup of tea and me some orange juice.

'What does he do?' Uncle Jack asked, not even noticing the steaming cup of tea.

'Everything. We gypsies can do almost everything.'

'Except say thank you,' Aunt Emma said primly, 'but then, it seems, neither can your Uncle Jack.'

'Thank you,' Uncle Jack and I said, all guilty-faced together.

'My brother Tashar is mostly into horses,' I told Uncle Jack, resting my chin on my hands and quite forgetting to drink. I didn't even listen to my own tumble talk. My mind was back in the past and I was riding with Tashar.

'I don't often go with Tashar,' I explained, 'but at Alfreton Fair, last year, something wonderful happened. Tashar lifted me up on to our great shire, as if I was light as a feather. Her name is Bryony. A gentle name, for a kind-hearted mare. She blew down her nose as I rose up in to the saddle. She always did that. It was her way of telling me that she was pleased to see me. I had my carry bag stuffed full of herbs and something very important to do. Usually, Tashar is not one to stay with a chavi, mostly likely he'll pretend I'm not even about.'

'I can't understand *anybody* getting away with ignoring you,' Uncle Jack said. He was wearing his teasing voice and I was glad it was Sunday and he had time to spare.

'Tashar's taller than my other brothers and clever-clogs smart. He's sort of king of our tribe. *Everyone* respects Tashar. He's taken over from our dad, even though some of my other brothers are getting wrinkle-skin old.'

'And he's your favourite too?'

'My mam says I should love them all equally. My mam says every one of them is kushti, but . . .'

41

I sighed, seeing Tashar reaching out for me from his Bryony throne. 'When he looks at me, with those star-shine black eyes, well, then I would follow him until my feet were bare shredded. He's a mighty fine Rom.'

'That's an awful lot of love for one brother,' Uncle Jack said, biting into some buttered toast and not noticing the drips, even though Aunt Emma gave him one of her mind-your-manners stares. The sort that makes you shiver-shrink to nothing.

I pointed to the butter drips and gave Uncle Jack a God-you-better-be-careful shrug. Uncle Jack just laughed and Aunt Emma stopped being a snooty snob and dug out some niceness. 'One day, you'll love another man like that.'

'Yeah, that's what my great-gran says. She warns me not to, bored-skull often. "Freya," she says, "don't waste all your time feather picking. There's more to life for you than a thick-skinned Rom. Why, on your own, you can achieve *anything*." '

'She sounds a bit like your mother!' Uncle Jack said to Aunt Emma, and she scowled at him. I don't think he had on his teasing voice.

'Did you enjoy your outing with Tashar?'

'Oh, Aunt Emma, it turned out to be a really exciting day. Tashar had been told about a horse. It was a piebald cob gelding, about fifteen hands high, with black and white patches. He said he was *beautifully* marked.

'My brother loved that horse, from the very first moment he saw him. My prala Tashar has a keen eye for horse flesh. I was almost too scared to ask why *I* was wanted. I longed so much to go to Alfreton Fair with Tashar. I was up-in-the-air excited. He said he *really* needed me.

' "Old Tom Brimble says the cob is going for a song," he said, "but it's got a nasty cough. Now you, my chime chick, are the expert on medical matters. If you can cure it we buy, if not . . . well, I expect it will be the knacker's."

'Oh, I felt so fizzle-burst happy. Tashar was going to listen to me. He was treating me as a proper grown-up person for the very first time.

'I raced over to our great metal wagon and gathered the herbs I might need. Tansy and burdock root for conditioning; elecampane and gentian to improve a poor appetite; feverfew, in case there should be signs of a cold; and finally, belladonna, a very dangerous cure for the most serious coughs of all. Belladonna is a kill or cure remedy. Only a Chime Child can use it safely.

'Within minutes, I was back beside Tashar, his arms were reaching out, lifting me on to Bryony, and I was the queen to his king.

'Alfreton Fair is one of Tashar's favourites. A lot of his friends live near by. Alfreton is best known for its shires. Our Bryony had been purchased there.

'When we arrived, the place was already full of chattering people and snorting horses. An old man leaned on a fence. Tashar raised his hand in greeting and I realised it must be the old man Brimble.

'Tom Brimble wore a threadbare jacket that was longer than his arms. His trousers were as dusty and wrinkled as his skin. I wondered if the clothes

43

had stretched with wearing, or the old man had simply withered. He smelled of pipe smoke and old cats. I tried not to breathe in his odour, and smiled politely.

' "You brought the lass then?"

' "The chavi can sense a good horse."

'I held my head high, feeling very proud indeed.

'The old man simply sneezed. I stared fascinated, as little dew drips glistened in his sparrow-pecked moustache.

' "Don't stare, child. I'll not bite thee."

'He wiped his face with the back of his grubby hand. I moved closer to my brother.

'Tashar laughed at my squeamishness. He was acting like *he* had no nose at all.

' "Got a few things to do, Tom, will you mind the chavi?" He didn't wait for an answer, one minute he was there, the next gone.

' "So you're good with the herbs then?"

' "My great-gran learned me."

' "Is that the one Tash calls Ostrich?"

'I nodded. Old man Brimble must be a very good friend indeed, if Tashar had told him *that*. I relaxed and we stood together, watching the world go by. There were bargaining people and waving arms everywhere. Horses were trotted and cantered. Feet and teeth were inspected, eyes peered into and legs rubbed. The place hummed with busy buying bodies.

'Over on the other side of the main square, I could see Tashar chatting to his friends. He obviously had no intention of letting on that the piebald close by was of interest to him.

44

'Near to Tom Brimble and I stood a flashy young man, holding on to a highly strung Arab mare. She was pure white, and butterfly dancing. The thresh of hot-mashed bodies was not to her taste at all.

'The young man was showing off even more than his horse. He was chatter-charming a pretty young woman who wore a frock that was supposed to be wedding white, but looked well-washed yellow when contrasted with the prancing Arab.

' "Bit skittish, that one!" muttered Tom Brimble and I wasn't at all sure whether he was referring to the frilly-frocked girl or the highly strung horse. He lit his pipe while I thought about it and sent billows of smoke in all directions. "They'll be trouble if he tries to ride her, mark my words, lass, they'll be trouble. Look how that mare rolls her eyes."

'I glanced at the old man. I was surprised he could see the horse, let alone the whites of her eyes.

'By now Tashar had left his friends and was heading back towards us. The old man was still watching the girl and the white Arab. He nudged me and I turned to see the snooty-faced girl being lifted high into the saddle.

'The highly strung Arab, made nervous by the girl's shrieks, was trying to throw her and she was clinging on to its reins for dear life. The likely lad had not sensed danger. His eyes were fixed on the girl. He made no attempt to calm his horse, just carried on telling the girl how lovely she looked. How he would like to be knight to her princess.

'The girl was trying to smile, but her face was pasty-patch white. She offered no soothing words to her mount. Her hands pulled hard on the reins, so hard that the bit was pulled tight in the poor mare's mouth and her feet climbed even higher towards the sky.

'Tashar was fair close now and I moved towards him. Just as we were about to meet, the white Arab snorted. Her back was bent almost backwards in her desperate efforts to escape the biting bit.

'In the same instant, the girl in wedding white flew into the air and her Romeo was felled by those frantic unbalanced hooves. He crumbled, still empty-head smiling, to the floor.

'Tashar leapt forwards, catching the girl in mid-fall. Instinctively, I reached for the reins of the panicking horse.

'I grabbed her reins and whistled softly through my teeth. I did it just like Tashar had shown me when I was years-ago small. I hissed and whistled, so low that the mare was reassured by my calmness. When she slowed to listen, I blew gently down my nose. She stopped steady to watch. I blew softly soothing huffing noises down my nose again.

'And suddenly, she stopped being scared and came to me. She sniffed gently at *my* nose. I stood still, holding her rein loosely, and whistled, whisper-softly. The magnificent white mare lowered her head and looked into my eyes. I noticed that *her* eyes were big and brown, with not a hint of rolling white.

' "Too fancy to work for a Romany," Tashar

said, reading my mind. "Can you see *her* hauling a wagon or dragging piles of wood?"

'I shook my head. My brother was right. The piebald cob, when cured, would serve us greatly well.

'Tashar took the reins from my hand and passed them to a friend of the injured young man. "Keep an eye on the boy," he instructed. "He looks fair winded to me, but maybe that's knocked some sense into his skull."

'He took my hand, ignoring the admiring look on the face of the girl in the dust-decked frock. "Fancy a drink to say thank you?" she asked, desperate to detain him.

'Tashar shook his head. "Go with your head-split boy. You're well matched, the pair of you. Both stupid."

'He led me off. My legs had to work scramble-toe fast to keep up with him. "Come, little sister," he said. "It's time for you to advise me. I wish to purchase a horse."

'I felt so proud,' I told Aunt Emma and Uncle Jack. 'There was this pretty girl in a fussy-feather frock, but he thought her silly and walked away with me.'

'Your Tashar is not one for the ladies then?' Uncle Jack asked, poky-nose curious.

'Oh, but he is! But not the simper-whimper variety. My great-gran says he'll grow into a rag-eared old tom-cat, unless a suitable chavi comes up and grabs his heart soon.'

'Well,' said Aunt Emma, as if she was not quite sure what to say next. 'Tell us the important thing.

After all that excitement, did you *actually* buy the horse?'

'After Tashar rescued the white-frocked wonder, he, Tom Brimble and I ambled over to look at the piebald.

'He was dull-coated, even though he'd had himself rubbed over with paraffin. His head hung low and his eyes were switch-light-out sad. On top of that, his feet hadn't been trimmed for weeks and he limped.'

'So you didn't buy him?'

'Tom Brimble, and Tash leaned against the fence and talked about having a little flutter later on. They took no notice of the piebald at all. Our Tash had no intention of being taken for a flat. There was no way that he would risk losing *his* reputation, not over a scruffy horse.

'I climbed over the fence, and approached the hoss. Oh, Aunt Emma, it was beautifully marked. There were big black and white splodges all over him, and he had one white foot.

> *One white foot, buy a hoss*
> *Two white feet, try a hoss*
> *Three white feet, shy a hoss*
> *Four white feet, shoot a hoss.*

'So you can see the piebald's patches were very well placed indeed and it was not surprising that Tashar had taken a shine to him.

'Old Tom Brimble and Tashar suddenly appeared to notice me. "Be careful, Freya, that horse looks a bit nasty to me."

'I ignored Tashar, put my hands behind my back,

and blew ever so gently down my nose, just like I do with Bryony.

' "Hey, lass, mind that brute don't kick you!" called Tom Brimble. "Not *too* close now."

'Again, I pretended I was muffle-ear-holed. I whistled softly through my teeth and held my head close to the piebald's face. I sucked up my nose and inhaled his scent. He smelt musty neglected, but not three parts dying. He smelt lots better than old Tom Brimble.

' "The germs that lass will catch!" muttered Tom Brimble, blowing clouds of black smoke all over Tashar.

' "Yes, her mam will go mad," Tashar agreed. "That horse has a real bad cough. She'll kill me if I take her home with that."

' "There's nothing wrong with Domino!" a tall thin man drawled, chucking his not-quite-dead fag-end down by his horse.

' "Are you blind, man? There's everything wrong with that ragbag on legs."

' "Yeah, he's for the knacker's all right," Tom Brimble said, nodding wisely and blowing out even more smoke.

' "I think he's *lovely*," I whined, rushing over to Tashar, dressed in my most pleading face. "You promised me a horse, yes you did, and I want *that* one."

' "Why?" old man Brimble asked, his face all gaped open in disbelief. "Of all the lovely horses here, you want that bag-o'-bones cob. You must be right out of your tree."

'I wiped a few grubby tears from my face. "He's poorly. Oh, Tashar, I'm sure I can make him well."

' "I told you she was a few fields short of a farm," Tashar told Tom, his voice all grumpy. "Come on, girl . . . home."

' "Make me an offer," the skinny man said. "*Poor* little girl."

'Tashar shrugged and rooted around in his pockets.

' "Don't be daft, boy!" said Tom Brimble.

' "Please. He's so sick and I'm sure I can make him better."

' "She thinks her name is Florence!" Tashar whispered loudly to Tom, as he pulled out a little pile of battered notes. He turned to the weasel man. "That's the best I can do, and a far sight more than the glue man will give you."

'The skinny man scowled. Tashar went to put the money back. "Suit yerself. Come on, girl, over there is a really pretty young filly."

'I looked to where Tashar and Brimble were pointing. After a while I mustered a smile.

'The thin man grabbed the money that Tashar had not quite managed to stuff in his pocket and pushed the piebald out of the pen towards me. Tom and Tashar took no notice. All man-chatter-tongued, they ambled off. I started to follow. Tashar turned. "*Your* horse, *you* feed it!" he said, and he sounded really cross.

'When we were safely away from the market, Tashar and Tom stopped rabbiting and waited for me to catch up.

' "Did I do well?"

' "Is the horse curable?"

'I nodded. "A spoonful of dried belladonna at the back of the tongue, a little chime magic, a rest and some food, and he'll be fine."

' "Then, little Chime Chick, you were brilliant."

' "One of the boys!"

'Oh, Aunt Emma and Uncle Jack, I felt like I had world-climbed to the stars. I was all itchy-skinned excited. They were *so* pleased with me, they let me come to the pub with them. They even bought me a pint.'

'Did you drink it?'

'No,' I admitted, my face screwing up so much at the memory, that both Aunty Emma and Uncle Jack laughed. 'It tasted horrid. I straight went out and fed it to the horse.'

6

'I am a Chime Child'

After I had given my baby bird yet another feed and washed my hands free of stinky bird smell, I wandered downstairs.

'Don't pick your nose, Freya!'

'Do you know someone called Sally, Aunt Emma?' I asked, in order to stop her paying so much attention to me.

'Yes, Freya. Why?'

I chewed on my nose-hooking finger and totally ignored her warning look. 'This Sally, is she going to have a baby?'

'Freya! Do not eat bits from your nose *ever*. It really is a quite disgusting habit.'

'My mam . . .' I saw Aunt Emma shudder, as if hardly daring to listen to my next offering. I decided to really impress her. 'My mam says if you chew greenies, then you don't get sick.'

'What?'

'You don't get colds and guts ache and things. You gets guarded.'

'Guarded?'

I shrugged. 'Doesn't matter! I wanted to tell you about Sally.'

'What do you mean, *guarded*?'

'Simple! Us travellers ... especially us proper travellers, don't get sick like you gorgio folk. We don't get ourselves poor-tummy ill if we eat something a teeny bit old. My mam told me that you have to eat a peck of dirt too, to make sure that you become extra well guarded. If you do all that, then the nasty germs can't catch you.'

'I suppose you have a point,' Aunt Emma admitted grudgingly. 'When I was a kid, it appeared to be the fussy mums who seemed to have permanently sick kids.' She gave me one of her long thoughtful looks. 'I have to admit that I thought the pampered kids were away sick because their mothers panicked every time their darlings sneezed. You know, Freya, I didn't like the posh kids much either, but when I grew up I discovered they were just like you and me.'

'No, they're not! They have lots of *things* and they get sick because they don't pick.'

'They're happy and sad, lucky and unlucky, just like us.'

'Not so lucky as me,' I said, grinning at Aunt Emma. 'I can run with no shoes. Well, I can when you're not about, anyway, and I have a silly soft-feather chíriko friend.'

'More lucky than me,' Aunt Emma said quietly and I knew she was thinking of the much-wanted baby that never came. My mam says babies are like bunnies, you gets none or hundreds, but never when you're really starving. No wonder Aunt Emma looks so thin!

'Oh, you'll be all right,' I replied, mind-sensing

the sad little thoughts in Aunt Emma's mind. 'My great-gran says that the best things in life are often those that surprise you. And my mam says everything comes to him that waits.'

'Freya, what rubbish are you talking now?'

I knew I should have to learn to be more careful. I'd nearly let my secret escape. My mam said I was never to let people guess that I had the gifts of a chime child, but my mam had deserted me, even though there was a very good reason. I felt that I'd earned myself the chance to impress. After all, for the moment, Aunt Emma was the nearest thing that I had to a mother!

I turned my thoughts to Aunt Emma's best friend Sally. 'You never answered my question! You never told me if I was right about Sally having a baby. Not that I'm overly fond of smelly babies, but I'm curious.'

'Yes, you *are* right about Sally having another baby. I was thinking of taking you over to meet her soon, but only if you promise not to pick your nose,' Aunt Emma said, with not even a hint of a smile. 'My friend Sally is having yet *another* baby, and though of course I wish her well, it's not fair, is it? It's not as if she's not *had* all the babies that a mother needs to have!'

Aunt Emma tried hard to hide her envy. She did it by putting on her teasing voice. 'That man of hers could easily have gypsy blood in him, his liking kids so much . . . you have to admit that it *is* unusual to want *so* many.'

I changed the subject. Aunt Emma was almost mind-thinking, besides, she sounded very jealous indeed to me. Goody-goody Aunt Emma felt sick as a pig at the very idea of Sally being pregnant. I was almost pleased to find out that she was as human as me. Somehow it made her nicer.

'Has Sally got brown eyes and a posh house too? Posher than yours?' I asked, knowing full well that she had, but just hoping to wind Aunt Emma up a little bit more.

'Yes. So don't you *dare* let me down with your dirty little habits. Remember, picking your nose, even if it does give you some immunity from disease, has to be done in private . . . if at all.'

'Like peeing?'

'Freya!' Aunt Emma tried to lead me back to nicer things. 'How on earth did you learn that Sally has a very expensive house? You must have eavesdropped. You really mustn't listen to other people's telephone calls, Freya. It's very rude.'

'I didn't listen to your stupid telephone calls, really I didn't.'

I felt cross. I knew my face held a sullen expression. I was innocent. I never listened to dull old telephone calls. Who needs telephones when you can sense-think. I decided that, perhaps, I didn't really like Aunt Emma, after all.

'I didn't earwig! I didn't! Just 'cause you can't have a smelly baby, doesn't mean I listen to tittle-tattle telephone calls!'

Aunt Emma was *very* angry now. 'You selfish child!' she yelled. 'How on earth can you know what it's like, not to be able to have the children you always dreamed of! How can you even *imagine*?'

I felt guilty. My eyes filled with proper tears. I'd hurt her when she was trying to be kind. I'd hurt her, just because in my head I was hurting too. My mam had, after all, found things to do that were more important than me. She had listened to the great-gran choviar (gorgio witch to you) and left me alone to do my very first magic.

It was *my mam* who had thought up the drúkkerébema. It was *her* fault that I had had to go away.

I felt very homesick. I wanted my mam and my great-gran, even if she was the biggest bossy-boots in the whole wide world. I wanted to sleep under the vardo. I longed to stare up at the stars in the cold silence of the night. I yearned to be wild-wind free.

I sighed. I am a Chime Child. I had been born to take responsibility. I repeated in my head the words that my great-gran had told me so often. 'Freya, with the gift of magic, comes the loss of freedom. Everything has a natural balance.'

Aunt Emma saw that I looked sad, and softened. 'I'm sorry, Freya, I know things are difficult for you, your mother just vanishing into thin air. It's just that some things are ... well, personal.' She was trying to be honest with me, attempting to cheer me up. Aunt Emma seemed to have a cold steel outside and a lovely jelly-soft inside, trouble was, it didn't always leak out when I wanted it to.

I longed to tell her the truth. I wished I could explain that I knew more about Aunt Sally than she ever dreamed. Even though Aunt Sally and I had never met. I really wanted to confide in her, but if I did that, then the magic wouldn't work. Aunt Emma was going to have to be even more sugar-spice nice if the drúkkerébema was to be fulfilled.

7

'Freya, you *must* go back!'

People in posh houses like shopping. My mam told me that and, sure enough, almost every morning we went shopping again. We bought curtains and cushions, skirts, socks and shoes, but never seeds. Always, there was too much to be done. 'Tomorrow, darling,' Aunt Emma would say, when I begged. 'I'm sure there will be time tomorrow.'

I felt tetchy-toed fed up, dead sure that the reason Aunt Emma wouldn't buy seeds was she didn't want to risk me spoiling her far too posh garden. Even Uncle Jack's cabbages all stood to attention and were exactly shaped round.

While Aunt Emma was busy choosing bread and cake for tea, I gave my baby bird a quick squirt of watered-down cereal to stop it squawking. Full-tummy satisfied, it settled itself back down in the bottom of my carry bag. It was as if it knew that that was the very best place to live. It fluffed up its feather spikes and promptly went to sleep. I swore it had grown mountains since yesterday.

'When can we go home?' I asked, bored as houses.

'Soon.'

It was always soon. I was full bothered with silly shops and endless buying. My tummy felt tearful trembly. I wanted my family: Tashar and Dibby, Mam and Great-gran, but mostly, I needed a little space to be me.

I waited until Aunt Emma wasn't looking and quickly slipped away. By the time she looked up and started to shout, I was hidden in scurrying shopping crowds. If I was lucky, me and my baby bird would vanish from her dreary life for ever.

Soon we would be free! We could go gathering wild things, berries, leaves, rabbits and hares. We would take just what we needed and not a bit more. We would live a proper natural life, instead of scurrying about on the surface. We would be part of things.

I wasn't scared to set off with just a small bird for company, not a bit. Sooner or later I would pick up a patteran and that would lead me to my family. Gypsies always leave road signs when they travel. Things that, to a gorgio, mean nothing. Our patteran signs are usually made from split sticks or clumps of grass, natural things that, to the untrained eye, seem to be left by chance.

I had no horse and no vardo. I had legs that were not-many-miles-fast-walking grown. I decided to start off the easy way. I made my way to the bus station. It was simple to find because it was just by the big precinct, where Aunt Emma liked to shop so much. It was big and crowded and full of mostly old buses. I asked which one went to Strawberry Woods and in no time at all I was settled on the top deck, all ready to go back to the place where my family had been, before they abandoned me.

I had told them that I wasn't ready to do my own magic yet, but they went and left me all the same. I would go back and tell them they were being stupid, expecting so much of a child like me.

I looked down from my window seat. Just as we were driving down the main street, I saw Aunt Emma was waving her hands like mad and a big policeman was trying to calm her down. A tiny bit of me felt awful, for causing her so much head-hurt. She looked scared to death. I nearly got off the bus and ran to her, but I wanted *my* mam, not stuck-up Mrs Hemmingway. She'd soon forget me. To her I was just another little orphan Annie. Someone would soon find her another one.

When I asked the conductor to let me off at Strawberry Woods, I held out my fare. He took nearly all the money that Aunt Emma had given me to spend. I realised there was no turning back. I didn't have enough money left for any more buses and it was far too far to walk, even on a lovely day like this. I would be lucky to buy even an ice-cream, with the few pennies that I had left.

I leaned back in my seat and tried not to think of Aunt Emma and Uncle Jack. I was a Romany and used to being free. It wasn't fair to expect me to grow posh manners and go shopping all day. I should be gathering fresh herbs with my mam and then drying them, all way careful, in the springtime sunshine.

My chíriko was beginning to break out in feathers. I took him out of my bag and looked at him real attentive, as we trundled along. The feathers were growing black with a hint of blue. I realised that my new friend was a thieving magpie. They were supposed to be unlucky, but I didn't care. I was sure they had to be safe if you rescued them.

My bold-eyed bird stared back at me, all friendly faced. The bus ride didn't frighten it at all. I reached down and stroked its little head. He gently held my fingers in his beak. It was as if he was telling me not to stop.

I was fed up with having a fledgeling with no name. All this time I had waited just to be full heart-sure that I knew what sort of feather-dressed bird it was going to be. I have three names, including a secret one that my mam whispered when I was born; so secret that she'll only tell me again when I am grown.

I have a wagon name. That's what my people call me. A wagon name is the same as a nickname, like you gorgios have but my wagon name is extra special. I'm called Chime. That's because I'm a seventh child, born on Good Friday as the clock struck twelve. I'm a chime child, born with special magic powers. I still don't know my secret name. Lastly I have an ordinary name. Freya, because I'm a Friday-birthed child.

As I sat on the big bus that was trundling me towards freedom, I decided to call my bird Maggie, an ordinary name for an ordinary bird. Everything should have a name . . . everything. I made up my mind, too, that Maggie was a girl bird. I have too many brothers. I think I like girls best. Last of all, I gave my bird a wagon name. I called her Kackaratchi, which is simply the Romany name for magpie.

I climbed down from the bus at Henberry Lane and headed off up the little hill path, that I recognised as soon as I saw it. Up and up I climbed, past the neat little houses on the edge of the town. Most had handkerchief gardens, all wearing their best springtime clothes. There were daffodils as far as the eye could see. They swayed in the wind, looking like a seasick seaside.

I stopped by one little house, near the end of the lane. Out in the front was a bit of earth that was jammed full of sweet-smelling hyacinth. Part of the garden was shaped like a waning moon and full of red, white and blue flowers. They were really bright and cheerful. I bent down to sniff and the stink was so strong it fair made me sneeze, but it was *lovely*. I picked myself a flower to keep and hurried on. It crossed my mind that the owner could be a didakai, liking such vibrant colours so.

Just further on from where the last house stood, on the narrow path that, in turn, led into the woods, I passed a couple, who looked *nearly* as old as my great-gran. They were walking out with a tiny dog. The dog had spiky fur stuck out over its eyes, and a pink ribbon in its hair. It looked like a shopping-counter, fluffy silk dog. The sort Aunt Emma and Uncle Jack might buy for their next dump-doorstep child, especially at Christmas time . . . if the orphan was really unlucky. Me, I prefer big scruffy wagging-tail dogs, with real deep barks, but I was as polite as Aunt Emma would have wished. I smiled and said good morning.

'What are you doing out all alone?' the old lady asked.

'Yes, surely you are too small to go into the woods by yourself,' the old man echoed.

'My gran's up ahead.'

I didn't really lie ... well, she might be there, after all. Strawberry Woods was a favourite stopping place, so I was hoping.

I longed to see them again, all of them, even flipperty-dipperty Gran, who was not quite all there. We all loved her dearly anyhow, especially Mam. My mam should never have been born, my great-gran said, not if things were right proper. She didn't *really* care, now she could love-boss us all: Dibby, Mam and my brothers and me.

Soon the last house was long since passed. Nearly naked beeches began to crowd round me. My spirits lifted and I started to sing. I was free! I was once more a woodland spirit. I didn't care that I was quite alone. Well, all except for my friend Maggie, that is.

The wood was still dressed in its winter blanket. The sun was hot and passed easily through the mostly bare trees. I scuffed through the carpet of crisp brown leaves that still had not rotted or blown away. I scuffed in my lovely bright shoes which I never wanted, but were perfect for scuffing.

If my family had been there, I would have had me a wagon dog to fetch sticks. Sabre was my favourite. He was big and brave and kept us all safe at night. He usually slept under Great-gran's wagon, as did Fusty and Woodpile, but he was the best. Often I slept under the vardo too, with just the dogs to keep me warm.

As Maggie and I walked up towards Strawberry Woods, I imagined how much nicer it would be if Sabre, Fusty and Woodpile were with me too.

Sabre, Fusty, and Woodpile are not just keep-your-toes-warm dogs. They can hunt and they do, but only on command.

My dad trained them. He made them grow from pups with ferrets for friends. That way, they can safely work together. My dad wasn't having his best working ferrets ending up as dog dinner.

Tashar mostly runs the dogs now. Once he let me come hunting too. It wasn't that he was being small-sister kind. It was just that he didn't want to be nagged by Great-gran. He wanted to be buddy-buddy boozing.

'Your mam has a craving for rabbit,' Great-gran said, 'and so for that matter do Dibby and I, so don't you dare disappear until the shoshi is ready for the pot.'

'But, Ostrich!'

'What son dares not care for his mother? Have you no sense at all? Now go! A poacher like you should not take a minute.'

'The others are already away. You expect me to lay nets quickly, on my own?'

'Can I come?' I had asked, eager to tag along.

'You? Shoshi bashing?'

Tashar looked as if he was about to tell me to stick to selling clothes-pegs, but then his face soft-ened as he changed his mind.

'OK, Chime Chick, but when we get enough, then I slip away and you take them home.'

I nodded. I had long ago learned that, if Tashar took me with him, there was a very good reason.

Tashar whistled for the dogs and I skipped along beside him.

'You'll do as you're told.'

I nodded, happy to obey, not many a young chavi gets to go hunting with her brother.

I wanted to make sure that there was rabbit for my mam. Our Tashar had a mind to up and disappear. I was as pig-head stubborn as my great-gran. If my mam should crave for shoshi stew and Dibby wanted to cook, then that was how it would be.

Sabre and Woodpile are bushing dogs, whereas Fusty, who is terrier-type small, works best with the ferrets. Sometimes he goes real deep into the depths of the warren. Our Tashar says he has more than once near lost him.

When we reached the start of the woods, we laid out the long nets, quickly and quietly, so as not to disturb. Only when we had cordoned off the escape routes did Fusty, Sabre and Woodpile get called in to work.

Sabre and Woodpile are big and fast. They can close an area real well and drive open-air shoshi to netted cover. Fusty is best at driving them out from the burrow. They're good dogs, they work as a team. They chase, but they never kill. Tashar does that, quick and clean. One day I might have to kill my own rabbit. Now Tashar has shown me how. Sometimes, when he hunts, he uses a catapult, but the nets are quicker.

We hunt for food, or goods, never for fun. WE ARE NOT BAD, JUST HUNGRY. Great-gran says that nature is there to provide for us all and it will, provided we respect it and never take too much.

We caught four rabbits that evening. Three to sell and one for the pot. Tashar reckoned that was as much as I could manage to carry anyway. He packed the nets up and left me to cart them home with the rabbits. The dogs would make their own way back, as usual. They would each drift back alone. A poacher is easily recognised if accompanied by eager dogs.

Great-gran would have been spitting mad if she'd known how far we had gone and that I came back all the way on my own.

The heart of our camp is Great-gran's wagon, it's the barrel-top kind. The paintwork is all happy red and the roof is fresh-grass green. Tashar, my brother, has the task of keeping it all cheerful. He paints it oh-not-again-Ostrich! often.

We're proper Romanies, bright colours are our favourites, so, despite the red bodywork, and the green roof, the hubcaps and metal underwork are all painted bright sunshine yellow. Great-gran's vardo is lovely. It makes you feel really good, even on grey winter days.

There's little wooden steps that prop up by the side of the yellow wheels. My great-gran climbs up these to reach her favourite I'm-going-to-watch-the-world chair. Usually the door, with its little net-curtained window, is open. Only on really shivery days does my great-gran sit inside.

My mam, Dibby and I live in a modern caravan. My mam says that Great-gran huffed plenty when, years ago, my dad upped and bought it. 'That's not a Romany home!' she stormed, but Dad said that it was better for the boys. In those days I didn't count, I wasn't even born.

Our caravan has an inside lavatory, so there's no need for a special toilet tent. It has a shower and a modern cooker. It's big and shiny grey. It's very nice, I suppose, but boring. I'm just like my great-gran, I really much prefer the vardo.

Dibby Gran made us all a real nice hotpot that night, even thinking of it made my tummy grumbly. I tried to forget about water-mouth shoshi stew, and switched my mind back to today.

I hastened my steps and, in no time at all, I reached Dewberry Pond. The big deep bit at the bottom end was best. I felt safe-home comfy. Often, at harvest time, we would camp there for weeks. We are proper Romanies. We keep us tidy and neat, so that most people just wish us well, even envy us sometimes. It is only lately, now modern travellers are beginning to try and copy us, that some folk have started to nag us to go away.

Nowadays, in a lot of places, we can only stop for a day or so, and only if we're quite alone. Still, as long as we have Great-gran's proper vardo, we're mostly welcome. My mam says that, when Great-gran dies and her wagon is burned, things will change. We shall just look like any other sort of traveller in our modern caravans; mumpers, didakai, anyone. She says that I shall be one of the last proper Romanies. Soon we shall be forced to stay in a house, and give up for ever our wandering ways. She's wrong! I'm going to be a proper Romany for ever!

It was lovely by Dewberry Pond. I took off my posh new shoes and tied them to my bird-house carry bag, so they should stay safe. The large willow dripped catkins like raining candles. The sun shone so brightly that it was reflected in the water. I was filled to the brim with being happy. I forgot to look for my mam and my dibby gran and my great choviar gran. I was just happy being me.

All around stood beech and willow. Catkin willow and mostly winter-tight beech. Only here and there had little buds burst to show spring-time green. It was early, not yet Easter, yet the day was as warm as July.

'It's a fool's spring!' my mam would say. 'It'll snow again soon, you jus' see if I'm not right.' I grinned. She was usually right, my mam.

Sun shimmers lit up the pond like Christmas glitter. I dunked my hand and the water felt warm to my skin. It was no good. I had to listen to my heart. I took off my clothes and folded them all neat. I hung up my bag with my shoes and went for a swim.

I'm a water baby. I couldn't resist, even though I knew that it wasn't properly safe to swim all alone. My mam has always warned me never to go skinny-dipping all by myself, but on this day I didn't care. I am Freya, chime child, Romany with a secret name that even I have not yet learned. The woods would be safe for me, me and my yet-to-learn magic ways.

I swam and the water felt cool to my skin. The sun bounced off tiny ripples and shone in my deep black eyes. I dipped and dived like the true wild otter, in this secret place that only real walkers find.

I knew that I was unfairly happy. Soon I got shivery cold and so I crept out of the water to dry.

Where the sun shone through the unleaved trees, celandines lifted their heads in greeting. I settled myself down on a carpet of fine yellow flowers and waited for my goosepimpled skin to dry. Here and there I rubbed myself hard with my hands, for now I was quite cold despite the shining sun.

Rushlings, waking again from their winter sleep, stood to attention in the edges of the shallows, like soldiers guarding the central deep. I felt safe with them there, even when, out of nowhere, I heard my mother calling.

'Freya, you *must* go back!'

I closed my eyes. I knew she wasn't there, not really. She was only awake in my mind, but, my goodness, she looked fearsome cross to me. She had her hands on her hips and her eyes were don't-you-dare glaring. Although she was wearing her clean white cooking apron, the only thing she really looked as if she wanted to eat was me.

'I didn't want to go!' I explained to her, feeling shaky-tummy trembly. 'I told you that I was too small for lonely magic. I can't help it if I got shut-in-house stuffy and lots-of-shopping sick.'

'That's no excuse! You're a chime child. It has to be you. You, after all, were chosen.'

'I want to be travelling with my own-folk people. If I stay here, all alone, I might never come back, like Dad and Gramp.' I found myself desperately trying to make her feel sorry for me, even though, if I was honest, I knew that I was perfectly safe with Aunt Emma and Uncle Jack. Bubble-over bored, but stone-castle safe.

'Freya, your gramp died of sickness, and your dad got killed poaching. Nothing like that'll happen to you.'

'They killed him!' I was losing. I was mind-talking drivel and my mam knew it. She was screwing up her pure white cooking pinny and wringing it round in her strong brown fingers. She was crease-happy cross, really she was.

'They never!' she stormed. 'He fell down a hole and got himself frozen, just as you will, skinny-dipping this soon in the year. Now go back. You are a chime child. Are you so brainless that you have forgotten so soon?

'*You* were born to work for your people. Now go back this minute. You have to earn the respect that your magic powers give to you. I tell you, *Freya, you must go back*! The fulfilling of the drúkkerébema depends on you.'

'I can't, I've spent all my pennies.' This time I was truth-telling. I'd lost the will to fight my destiny. If I was full-heart honest, I felt baby-ashamed of running away so soon. Even Maggie-Magpie was beady-beam cautious. Her head was tilted on one side as she watched me. She looked as if she thought she knew *exactly* what I should do.

'Walk back to Henberry Lane then. We'll wait for you there,' my mam ordered, throwing her rag-wrung pinny on to the stony ground.

I sighed. I might have Romany magic, but my mam has an I'll-spank-you tongue. I reached out for Maggie, who fluffed up her feathers as if she was trying to say *I told you so*!

My mam, who wasn't really there, was miles mind-back gone. She'd had her word say, and now she was waiting for me. I had no option but to do as I was told.

The sun was beginning to cool. I climbed back into my clothes. No matter where I ended up, I knew my mam would find me. I wasn't scared.

Patterans are not necessary with really *close* family. Finding someone does not always mean following signs. It was easy for my mam to keep up with me. She had been very keen to trust me with our talking crystal and, up to now, I had wondered why. I should have guessed. It was so she could poky-nose pry. My mam might not have the powers of a Chime Child, but she still has ways of making sure I'm sensible.

Romanies know when someone has need of them. Even if the person themselves think they're doing fine alone. My mam was right. I couldn't hide out in Strawberry Woods for ever, sooner or later I would have to face my future.

I gave Maggie an extra big tummy feed to reward her for waiting, so quiet, for so long and, when she was full-feeling happy, I started the journey back home.

The vardo, our proper wagon, was already there, waiting at the end of the lane. Brightly painted it greeted me, and so did my mam and my great-gran and even Dibby Gran, who was the one to smother me with not-greatly-wanted wet kisses. They weren't cross-faced at all. It's the Romany way to up and leave, sometimes we must all take a little body space. They just needed to remind me that I had a job to do.

Bryony, our great and gentle shire, usually pulled the vardo; but, as they had hurried, Domino, the piebald gelding that I had cured with belladonna, was there too, acting as a sider. Now he was better, his coat shone. He could pull real well for a back-up horse.

Bryony blew down her nose in greeting. I whistled softly through my teeth and reached up to rub her velvet soft nose. Domino snorted. He was determined not to be missed out. He raised his lucky white sock and gently pawed the air, just to make quite sure that he had been seen. I hugged him too.

'Come on! We haven't got all day.'

Needless to say, it was my bursting-busy-mouth Ostrich gran, who was loud-mouth calling for a bit of hurry.

'I'm coming.'

'Too right, you are!'

I grinned as I climbed up and settled myself down, next to my mam. Nothing had changed. They were still waggy-tongued wonderful. I felt like a queen, as we trotted back to the town. Some folk waved. We were a pretty sight on such a sunny day. I love being a Romany. I love the clipping hooves and creaking wheels. I love the open air and even nagging old Mam and my dibby gran, who loves everything and everyone.

Despite her bossy-boot ways, it's especially cross-patch Great-gran I care for. We, after all, share the bond of secret magic. I feel heart-string tied; so much, that I could explode with caring. Here in the vardo, with my family, I am lock-heart tied and happy. I never ever want to leave, but as Great-gran says, nothing in life is that easy.

All too soon, I was dumped back into the gorgio world. My mam sternly reminded me that a chime child has to be big and brave, so I better start learning how. I would've been upset, but I saw an escaping tear in my mam's eye. It told me that she would cry as soon as I was safely out of sight, even if she did get a lecture from grumpy Great-gran.

I stood at the end of the road and waved, as our proper wagon faded into the distance. There in the back, Great-gran would be huddled in her bright comfy blankets, giving my mam some lip on the way that she drove.

'Too fast. You'll have us over, you'll wreck this wagon. Be careful! Hours and hours it took to do the carving on this vardo. It's worth its weight in gold.'

'Not to you, it isn't.'

'Of course it is! There's only a few left now, proper round wagons.'

'So why burn it then? Why, when you die, can't you leave it to me, like is now common? Or, even better, why can't you leave it to Freya?'

'When I go, I shall be burned in my wagon proper! If you want a wagon, then you get one of your own!'

'What shall I buy it with? Clothes-pegs and old lace?'

'Sell that stupid metal shed of yours! That's what!'

I laughed to myself as the wagon shrank into the distance. I didn't have to mind-read *that* conversation. It was *always* the same. Reluctantly, I watched them leave. Dibby was waving her handkerchief to make sure that she was the very last to be seen.

I slipped down the garden path and let myself in through the open gate. Aunt Emma could see I was safely back. I didn't say sorry and she didn't bother to point out it was well past my bedtime, or that I'd scared them half to death. She took the walking telephone into the kitchen to moan about me to her friends, while she had a nice cup of tea with Uncle Jack. As she went she told me to go to bed and wait for her there, but I didn't. She should have been angry, not calm. She should have cuffed me and cared.

I went back outside. I stayed in the garden until it was well past dark and still she didn't come for me. I was furious. She couldn't care that much if she let me stay out in the shadows. I decided that it was time to make her very cross indeed.

I took off my sunshine shoes and dipped my feet

in the pond. Then I found a nice muddy patch and jumped in it. I swirled the dirt about until my feet were all muddy black, right up to the top of my ankles. Satisfied that she'd really go mad, I marched indoors.

'Take your shoes off, Freya,' Aunt Emma said calmly.

'Not wearing none!'

'Take your feet off, Freya!'

I looked at her. She was not smiling and she was not shouting.

'Take off your feet, Freya.'

'That's silly!'

'No more silly than my expecting you to be grown up enough not to run away, or sensible enough to wash your feet, or wear shoes. No more silly than my hoping that I won't have to clear up after you as if you were a pet dog, and not the intelligent Romany child you claim to be.'

Suddenly I felt really silly. I had behaved like a great spoiled brat and deserved the lash of her tongue. She who had been so kind to me . . . even if it was because she couldn't have a blood-baby of her own.

'I'm sorry.' The words were stuck-throat hard to say, but I meant them deep inside.

'I'm sorry too and disappointed. I really believed that we had begun to get on well.' Aunt Emma's voice was chatter-teeth chill. I realised that she was fighting to control a bubbling pot of fear, mixed with anger. She half turned away, and then she twisted herself to face me again. Her body was bean-pole rigid and her clenched fists were glue-stuck to her sides.

'Uncle Jack was so furious with you. Especially when you walked in, calm as you like, with no mind to the trouble you have caused. He was so cross that he had to go off for a walk in order to calm down.' Aunt Emma's voice stopped being cold and just went sad. 'I've never known him to do that before. Not ever. You let us down, Freya. We trusted you.'

I rushed into my bathroom so that she wouldn't see the big tears filling my eyes. I scrubbed myself clean, hoping that she would be really impressed. I even scrubbed behind my ears, so potatoes couldn't grow. Aunty Emma didn't come to see, though I could hear her pottering round downstairs.

I climbed into my soft warm bed and waited for her to kiss me goodnight, as she always did. I waited a long time. I cried properly bad. I wanted my mam and my great-gran. I wanted Dibby Gran and her great slobbering kisses, I even wanted my prala Tashar.

I wished I was out in a starlit field kissing our hosses goodnight, or sat up in the proper wagon playing mystery games in the secret trails of blue that traced the deep red carpet. I wished I was anywhere but here.

Eventually, I heard Aunt Emma climb the stairs. I couldn't let her see how upset I'd been. I snuggled down in my comfy bed, clutched my teddy and pretended to be fast asleep.

Aunt Emma kissed me gently on the cheek. I didn't move a muscle, not one.

'I'm sorry I was so cross,' she whispered. 'I was so scared, Freya darling, when you ran away. I thought you were gone for ever.'

I peeped out from under my lashes. Aunt Emma had tears in her eyes too. I felt ashamed. I made up my mind never to run away again.

I suppose Uncle Jack came to kiss me goodnight. I hope he did. He's never missed before, even if he worked lots-time much. I don't know for sure. I cried myself to sleep. I clung to my well-worn teddy and sobbed and sobbed. I was so very ashamed for being bad.

It wasn't until morning that I learned how the police had searched for me for hours. My social worker had been properly mad too, when I turned up large as life and smiling. Offered to take me away she had, and said that I might be better behaved if I was placed where I could be kept more secure.

I deserved it. My mam would have clobbered me real hard, if I'd caused her such troubles. She'd have knocked me to hell and back for scaring her so.

It was only when I heard them arguing about me, that I realised that I'd had them heart-stop scared. So scared, that they never really believed I'd come back alive.

I was ever so grateful when Aunt Emma and Uncle Jack convinced the social worker that I should be allowed to stay. So grateful, that I unbuttoned my mouth and told them so.

8

'Babies is awful'

Aunt Emma found Maggie and me by the pond as usual. It was my favourite place to play. I could pretend I was back in camp with my family. If I was full-heart honest, although Aunt Emma and Uncle Jack were strange-child-kind and had given me toys and clothes and lots of love, I still longed to be home.

A sticky brick house, even if it is full of things, is still a cage. Sometimes I felt pit-stomach sad. I even pined for my noisy brothers, well, the two of them who haven't gone off to live with other gypsy tribes because they are silly enough to want to have babies and things.

I was only being long-distance loopy. My brothers are usually far too busy-bee-doing to find time to play with me anyway. Sometimes even a little Romany can have an attack of upset empty heart-sick!

I love Aunt Emma's secluded wild garden. Here, I can feel free to think about Mam and Dibby Gran and my great-gran. In my misty mind, I can be safely back with my family. It's nice to sit dreaming away with my feet in the water, so I was not best pleased when Aunt Emma came along to bring me back to the gorgio world.

'If Mrs Plumpton could see you now, with your feet in the pond, she'd be quite shocked.'

'I'm only swirling my toes. Cool toe-dibbling does no harm. The vicar's wife must be churchmouse scared, if I can spook her by just sitting here. She surely frightens herself easy, doesn't she, Aunt Emma? She must be a real baby-brain.'

Aunt Emma tried to look shocked. She tried ever so hard but she couldn't do it. She giggled. She did! Grown-up Aunt Emma giggled like she was only as big as me. When she giggles Aunt Emma looks quite pretty, even if she is prim and pertly painted to cover the cracks in her heart.

'Big baby!' I said, laughing to show her that I was pleased to see her so amused. 'Big baby!'

'And I thought you didn't like babies,' Aunt Emma teased. 'Sally is due to have her seventh next month. Imagine that lot! The oldest three are girls. You're bound to make a friend there and, of course, there'll be the new baby to cuddle soon.'

'Babies is awful. They cry, they smell and, worse of all, they pee all over you and, if they doesn't do that, they puke!'

'Freya!'

I was up to my ears in enjoyment. I loved baiting Aunt Emma. 'Anyway, you're wrong, the baby was born yesterday. It's a boy. Boy babies are even worse than girl babies, if you ask me. They cry more and they pee further.'

'Freya, you must mind your language! It is not becoming.'

'My mam says they do pee further, so there, and my mam has *hundreds*, so she should know!'

I'd earned another look of disapproval. Aunt Emma was obviously convinced that I was very rude and lying through my back teeth. I felt better! That would teach her not to believe me. I grinned at her like a Cheshire cat. My black eyes glinted as I dared her to shout.

'Babies is awful! My mam had *millions*, so *I should know*!'

'Freya, *please*!'

'Anyhow, your friend Sally HAS had her seventh child, so there. I'm a Romany so I know them things.'

'I'm sure your mam would be quite shocked at your wild imagination.'

To my surprise, Aunt Emma wasn't shouting. I think she was too busy working out what to say next.

'She's had the baby. *Honest*! Born the proper way it was, real quick. No messing!'

Now it was me struggling not to laugh. I kept my face straight and stared into her puzzled eyes. I could tell that she was starting to wonder if she should believe me. Her face was all screwed up and her eyes were patchy puzzled.

If I hadn't mentioned Sally, I think we'd have had yet another day of endless shopping, but now Aunt Emma was unsettled. She was smiling, but not inner-ear listening. Her mind was on with my telling her about Sally and the new baby. Even though her gorgio head told her she shouldn't *really* believe me, she wasn't feeling quite certain.

She wondered whether I'd gleaned half an idea from somewhere.

She bustled about in her nice neat kitchen, humming that odd little tune that tells the whole world that something is rattling round in her head. My dibby gran hums a tune like that all the time but that's because she can't remember what she should be doing, not until my mam tells her for at least the hundredth time.

Anyway, the shopping was quite forgotten. I went back upstairs to collect a little dish to feed Maggie and when I came back, Aunt Emma was still huff-puff humming.

'You're cross because you don't believe me!'

'I'm perfectly happy and I'm making you a nice liver casserole,' Aunt Emma said, but her back was bean-pole stiff, because she didn't even want to *think* that a little Romany might know more about her best friend than she did.

I decided to pay her back for not trusting my mind-thinks.

'I bet your stew is not as good as my gran's. Nobody can make a sastra pot like her! My gran is as dibby as ducklings, but she can make a stew that tastes better than *any* of that packaged stuff, no matter how many pretty pictures there are on the front.

'The first thing my brothers want, when they visit us, is some of Dibby Gran's special stew. All nicely flavoured with fennel, marjoram, wild thyme and, best of all, the secret things that only our dibby gran knows – and my mam says that it's probably best that way! I can't wait to see if Maggie likes her sastra pot too.'

'Freya, you are the most ungrateful little beggar that I have ever met!'

'I'm not a beggar!' I thumped my fists hard down on the table. 'We doesn't beg! We *sells*!'

'Freya, I didn't mean to even suggest that you did! I meant it as a term of affection. You really *must* try to be a little less sensitive. Now come on, taste this.'

I looked at her face. She didn't smile or frown. She simply held out the spoon for me to taste. I could read in her eyes that she meant me no harm.

'It's not bad! Not as good as Dibby Gran's, but then you can't get her special herbs, can you? It's not bad for a gorgio.'

'Praise indeed!' Aunt Emma said dryly.

Maggie and I retreated to the garden. It was another nice warm spring day. The sort that makes the grass smell extra nice. I decided that I would give my smelly little bird a nice warm bath. It was getting messier in feeding all the time. After each sticky mouthful she would shake her head spitting gluey gunk over anyone that was close, and that, was mostly me. The feeding had worked though.

Maggie had already grown bigger and stronger. She had sprouted black and white feathers that were magpie smart.

Not so good, though, was the tantrum temper that my kackaratchi chíriko had grown along with her fancy-fine feathers. She used it whenever she could, especially if I got things wrong, so they were not exactly as she liked.

Magpie was worse than my great-gran at strop-
ping to get what she wanted. If I ignored her
wishes, then she fizzy-fitted real good; and that
was the way with her bath.

I carefully put down her bowl and checked that
the water had cooled enough. I tested the water
using my elbow, just as my mam did when we
were small. When I was quite sure that I had done
things just right, I placed my little magpie down
beside her bath, quite certain that she would have
wet-feather fun.

I didn't have any worries about her escaping,
because the wild garden was quite big and, anyway,
she still couldn't fly properly. She tried, she flapped
her wings and things. She flailed them as fast as
she could, but not even her little feet lifted from
the ground. It made me laugh to watch her try and
that made her very cross indeed. She feather-flap-
ped even harder and squawked in temper.

The day I'd gone itchy-feet walking and upset
the gorgios so, I had given her a name. I had called
her Kackaratchi-Kackaratchi, that is, Maggie-
Magpie, even though I knew that, one day, she
should go free. Magpies are unlucky if kept against
their will. A named magpie is harder to part with,
then it's like losing a pet. In my heart of hearts, I
hoped that Magpie was getting tame. I wanted her
to choose never to leave.

For a long time nothing happened, except for
Aunt Emma peering out at me from the kitchen
window. Luckily, she never called and spoiled
things. She was just worry-checking that I was safe.
All the time my fat little magpie bird watched the

bowl and watched me, but she didn't *do* anything. I sat, fisherman-still, like you do by a stream, or in the woods when watching for deer. I was plenty poaching patient.

> *'One for sorrow*
> *Two for mirth*
> *Three for a wedding*
> *Four for a death . . .'*

I softly sang the song that my great-gran had taught me and Maggie-Magpie seemed soothed. She lifted a foot over the edge of the bowl and tested the water.

The water level wasn't right! Magpie threw the most magnificent temper! She flapped her wings and squawked in anger. She did a war dance all round her bowl. Hopping and shrieking, she was. I found myself struggling not to laugh. My face was all tightly screwed with not giggling. Animals get upset if you mock them . . . just like people do.

I tipped a little of the water on to the grass and wondered if it was getting too cold for a bath anyway. Magpie inspected the water again. It was still too deep. She hopped back on to the grass and cussed me. She threw her feathers about and stomped and huffed, as only a stroppy magpie can.

I tried really hard not to splutter-smile. You should never upset a magpie. They can bring you sorrow, if upset, and then you have to turn three times round and spit over your left shoulder twice, so as to make things right. It was not too difficult to do, but I couldn't be bothered. I smothered my grinning.

Now the water only reached halfway up her little black legs. I thought it was not fun-filled deep, but she thought it was wonderful. She stopped trying to deafen the neighbourhood, especially Mrs Plumpton, and settled down to doing some serious bathing.

Each time her little pudding body dipped into the water, her expression changed to one of delight. She flapped and splashed for ages. She threw water at all her feathers, even gathering water up in her beak so that she could clean right under her newly feathered wings.

Aunt Emma would have been impressed with Maggie-Magpie's washing. She never left out a tiny bit. Aunt Emma was always telling me off for not changing my knickers, or washing my neck properly. I looked back towards the house to see if she was watching us, but she wasn't. I expect she was cleaning and polishing, just in case someone should really care whether there was a speck of dust here and there in her great big nearly empty house.

Maggie-Magpie looked a fine mess after her bath. Her body had shrunk to tiny again, with no fluffed-up feathers, and she was shiver-shaking with cold. I wrapped her up in one of Aunt Emma's nice warm towels and took her indoors to dry properly. Anyway, I thought that it was best to go in. I was sure that, sooner or later, we would suddenly have to stop for something urgent and forgotten and Maggie would have to be carry-bag dry.

I had to make sure, too, that my bird bag was all clean and comfy and her food packed all tidy.

That way, Magpie was safe and I could sneak her a feed if she got hungry. Aunt Emma wasn't really too happy about a magpie tagging along all the time. She pretended she wasn't there. She could only do that if the carry bag smelled nice and clean, looking as if it contained proper school books or something.

Oddly enough, Uncle Jack had quite taken to Maggie-Magpie. Every day he asked me how much she had grown. He even helped me to make a chart, so that I could record her weight each day, and how long her feathers had grown. He told me that he had a baby bird once, but it died. His face looked really sad when he memory-shared about his own child-time fledgeling.

His mam had held a lovely funeral, with a nice cross and a prayer and everything. My mam would do that too, but she'd feel in her heart that it was all unnecessary. She would say that all of us should be happy with the days that we are given. Animals, birds, gypsies and gorgios, all of us.

Every night, before my bedtime story, I liked to tell Uncle Jack about my day. Things like buying sunshine shoes, or how Maggie-Magpie had learned to eat tiny white worms from the compost heap. How she started by snatching them from my fingers and ended up digging them out for herself.

Uncle Jack got quite worried once, when I told him how Maggie had nearly eaten the little red beads that fell all over the bedroom floor when my necklace broke. He said it would be a real shame if she got herself ill, after all my getting up at nights.

I liked Uncle Jack coming to kiss me goodnight. Even if it was very late when he came home sometimes, and so Aunt Emma tut-tutted because I should have been sweet-dream sleeping, and not waiting for a man that didn't know when to leave his office. I'd not had a man pay me so much fuss for a long time. Not since I lost my dad.

Tashar tries sometimes, but he's rather like Uncle Jack. He usually has more important things to do. Vashti, who's much older than my prala Tashar, is even worse. He's magpie-minded, is Vashti. He's got collecting things fiddle-fixed deep into his brain. My mam has to nag him no end to keep things tidy. Sometimes she nags even worse than Aunt Emma!

That night, even after Uncle Jack had crept up to kiss me goodnight, I found it impossible to sleep. I lay snuggled up like a gorgio girl, but I longed to be one with the earth and the sky. I held the teddy Dibby had given me crooked under one arm and pulled the linking crystal from beneath my pillow, but still the sandman wouldn't come and neither did my mam. I felt as if more than our bones were apart. I was simply a lonely tear, shining among a thousand shimmering stars.

9

'Tea on the lawn'

'We're having friends round,' Aunt Emma told me cheerfully, 'so there are a lot of jobs for you to help me with today.'

'What sort of friends?'

'Acquaintances,' Uncle Jack said drily, biting into his morning toast.

'Well, all right, acquaintances, but I hope that they will become friends. Our new vicar, the Reverend Plumpton, and his wife, and Philip and Sandra from next door.'

'Is *that* why you were extra polish-perky yesterday and why we had to do such mountains of shopping?'

'Not *mountains*,' Aunt Emma said, sounding, I think, a trifle short.

'Yes, *mountains*,' Uncle Jack agreed. 'My wallet still hurts.'

'As it's such a promising day,' Aunt Emma added quickly, 'I think we might have tea on the lawn.'

I felt hip-hop happy. *Tea on the lawn*, now *that* was almost like being a Romany.

'Can Magpie come?'

'Certainly not!'

'But it's *outside*.'

'That smelly magpie stays in your room until the very last visitor is gone. Is that clear?'

Aunt Emma was wearing her see-how-stern-I-can-be face and I knew then that tea on the lawn was not in the least bit like being a Romany.

After a duster-drudge exhausting day, I was sent upstairs to settle Magpie into her carry bag, and then to wash and change into my very best frock.

The dress had far too many frilly bows. I felt small-girl silly. Aunt Emma had insisted it would suit me nicely. It didn't. It wasn't even sunshine happy. It was rose-bud pink. I *hated* it.

Aunt Emma spent hours dressing. Uncle Jack had to change his tie *three* times. We were all pink-faced scrubbed and, after all that, the tea party was boring.

I had spoken to Philip and Sandra from next door before and they were usually all right, but then they were wearing run-about clothes. Now they appeared full-feather dressed and, this time, they spoke in posh voices and weren't any fun at all.

Everybody hung about nervously. Aunt Emma's fingers were screw-twisted tight. Everyone obviously thought that the Reverend Plumpton and his wife were very important. I wondered if you had to curtsy, like to a queen. Aunt Emma hadn't *said*.

The vicar arrived in a black suit and a dog collar. Mrs Plumpton wore a full fussy frock that didn't make *me* feel quite as bad. She had almost as many fancy buttons as I had bows. We all looked so strutting-peacock silly that I just wanted to hyena-laugh out loud.

We all sat outside on Uncle Jack's perfectly neat lawn, in the perfectly neat garden. We ate cucumber sandwiches, with all the crusts cut off, and then all carefully cut into neat little triangles. Aunt Emma had made one of her really light sponges and filled it with strawberry jam and cream . . . that, at least, was finger-licking good. To drink, we had lemon tea in tall glasses, or chilled white wine. I was sulky-face stuck with the lemon. Aunt Emma said I was far too young to taste wine.

I practised making polite conversation, like Aunt Emma said I should.

'I have a magpie.'

'Have you, dear? How nice.'

'It's good fun.'

'That's nice.'

I wanted to say, *it squarks and it flutters and it shits all over the house if you let it*, just to see what happened. I opened my mouth.

Aunt Emma gave me one of her don't-you-*dare*-spoil-things looks, so I tied up my toggle-tongue and swallowed instead. I sipped the horrid lemon tea and bit into another cucumber sandwich. Aunt Emma rewarded me with a gigantic smile.

'It's a real bird,' Uncle Jack told our guests, 'and I expect Freya needs to go and feed it.'

Aunt Emma and Uncle Jack exchanged glances. Aunt Emma nodded. I realised that gorgios have a non-speaking language too.

'If you need to feed your magpie, then you may leave the table, Freya.'

I was fall-over-feet eager to go, but I minded my manners. 'Excuse me, please, Magpie needs to be fed. I'm sorry that I have to go and tickle-pink pleased that I have been allowed to meet you.'

I gave them all a very friendly smile, feeling quite proud of my giant white lie. Tea on the lawn was not even close to my idea of a good-girl treat. I turned to go back indoors. I was great-grin grateful to Uncle Jack. I wondered if he hated tea on the lawn too.

'What a *nice* child,' I heard Mrs Plumpton say. 'Is she your only one then?'

'She's my foster-child, Mrs Plumpton,' Aunt Emma admitted, 'but you're right. She's a very nice child indeed.'

Maggie-Magpie was flap-feather pleased to see me. I fed her some stew from a jar and told her she was lucky not to have to eat cucumber sandwiches. She squarked in agreement and stuffed herself until she was fat-tummy full.

Satisfied at last, she hopped on to my shoulder. We stared out of the window, watching the grown-ups talking quietly on the lawn. I was sure they couldn't *really* be having fun.

I lay down on my bed and Maggie-Magpie tucked up her feathers and nuzzled under my chin. We were both shut-eye sleepy. Her, from eating so much, and me, from slog-about-house business. Hidden under my pillow, as usual, was Mam's linking crystal. I closed my eyes and, in no time at all, I had mind-travelled home and a little way back in time.

'I've brought someone to see you . . . a didakai.'

My very big brother Vashti has a bellow-boom voice. It rang loud and clear across the camp, even though he was still hidden among the trees.

Mam stopped scrubbing clothes and raised her head. I ran outside, pleased to have an excuse to escape the helping.

'Come and see,' Vashti called, as if not coming was the end of the world. 'Look who's here! Our very own poshrat has come to visit us.'

Vashti emerged from the wood and with him was a stranger. Tashar left his horses and ran towards them. Mam forgot all about her clothes and rushed out with Dibby Gran. Even Great-gran, who was sleepy-eyed from her afternoon nap, peered down from her vardo with interest.

'Hi, Ostrich!'

'Hi, Poshrat! Seen sense and come to your people then?'

The stranger laughed, a deep rich laugh that was similar to Vashti's. 'Everyone is my people, Ostrich. I'm not as clan-minded as you.'

'Everyone or no one,' Great-gran said tartly, but the others ignored her.

'This is my Uncle George,' Mam told me, 'and this, George, is Freya. Why, she was only a baby when you saw her last.'

Uncle George picked me up and lifted me high in the air, like I was gossamer heavy. He gave me a gorgio kiss in greeting. I stared at him, fly-catching mouth-gaping. He wore black trousers, a wide belt and a big gold earring. Not only that, his shirt was far too happy bright for a gorgio.

'You stopping?' Mam asked.

'You cooking?' the poshrat replied.

Mam nodded and tried not to look pleased when he gave her a hug.

'I'm stopping.'

That settled, the men sat down to gossip and the women got cooking-pot busy. They did *not*, however, plan tea on the lawn.

Dibby made a sastra pot, with wood pigeon, turnips, wild thyme and garlic. Oh, and, of course, her secret things that no one likes to talk about.

Mam made a pile of buni manridi. I was mouth-water pleased. I have always been fond of her honey cakes.

Sometimes I go with Tashar on a honey raid. My herbal smoke tells the bees to lie real quiet. We only take a few frames and we always replace them with empty ones. Bees like to be busy, it gives them more space to work and, anyway, that way nobody knows that we've been.

I always thank the bees when we leave. You have to tell the bees everything. Otherwise they might fly away with your luck.

I did my bit too. I prepared the baked potatoes and even made sweet biscuits, using some more of the fresh spring honey. We all were bounding busy. My mam must be very pleased to see the poshrat George.

Tashar left the others to rokker and hunted about for dandelion wine and beer. In no time at all, it was time to eat.

We all had our own wooden bowls for the stew, except Poshrat George, who was given a bowl with

93

a visitor sign. Some were polished chestnut and some sycamore. Tashar had made them each one different, for that is our way.

Great-gran was served first. She is ancient-bold old and therefore the most honoured person, even though it was Poshrat George who had triggered the celebration in the first place.

We ate and drank and laughed, even I was allowed to join in and drink wine. Soon we were more than a little tingle-tongue relaxed and everybody was smiling.

Mam served up yet more honey cakes and stopped close to talk to Uncle George. 'It's not often we have the pleasure of seeing you, kokko. Not often that you step out of your gorgio nest. Now tell me, what *exactly* do you want this time?'

I snorted and nearly choked on my wine. Uncle George's grin spread from ear to ear; and my mam has the *nerve* to say that my great-gran is too jump-in-up-to-your-neck honest!

Kokko George took no offence at all. He just laughed out loud.

'We'll never make a gorgio of *you*, Lena.'

I listened even more wide-ear loud. I had never heard my mam called Lena, not by family. Everybody *always* called her Mam.

'Well?'

'Lena, I'm here to ask you a favour. I want you to use your influence on that great stubborn Ostrich. I need a drúkkerébema.'

'A drúkkerébema is not lightly given.'

Uncle George nodded and reached out for another buni manridi. 'I'll explain later and then,

I'm sure, you'll feel you can beat the old Ostrich into submission.'

Mam shrugged and went on to nudge Vashti with her foot. 'Do we get some music then?'

Tashar grinned and poked our prala too. 'Come on, Vashti, show the poshrat here what music *really* is.'

Vashti picked up his violin. He tucked it under his chin and, in that moment, his heavy body vanished. His arms performed a delicate echo of the music in his mind. My big boom-mouth brother *became* the very music he played. His head tilted over to one side and his eyes closed in sheer sensuous enjoyment.

Without words, Mam, Dibby Gran and I linked arms and began to dance. Slow gentle movements that breathed with the haunting sounds that Vashti played.

Tashar, too, felt his toes tingle-tap. He grabbed George and pushed him into the circle. The pace of Vashti's music was growing ever faster. Even Great-gran felt the call of the wild and had to join in. When Vashti played, all grumpy gripes were forgotten. The only thing that existed was the haunting sound. We *were* the dance, even Poshrat George, who had almost no music head at all.

Vashti was lost in his music mind. Louder and faster he played. Quicker and higher we danced. I felt myself being swirly sucked into the string wind-music. I became the leaves rustling in the trees and the stream water tumbling over the rocks. I was whisper soft and rushing wild. I *am* the spirit of the woodlands and the very salt of the earth. My great-gran has always insisted so.

We were all the dance, born to share the moon magic with nature's bright spirits, but I am a chime child too, so a bit of me is ever just a little alone. Sometimes I *am* the vibrating strings, or the beat of the drum, or the brilliant twinkling star.

Oh, was wild-wind *wonderful*, that night. Skirts and petticoats flashed. Earrings tinkled. Men and women laughed out loud, in sheer enjoyment. We danced for hours. Despite the many dancing feet, there was only one violin and one beating heart.

Great-gran gave in first. She limped back to her vardo and sat down on her in the door chair. She lit up her little clay pipe and smiled with pleasure. She was happy. It was like the old times.

The smoke smell from Great-gran's pipe mixed with that from the dying fire. The night air cooled, but the fever of the music kept us warm. We were all three parts motto and cared for nothing, except the mood of the music. The sky held a hint of morning and *still* we danced.

It was only after Mam's Uncle George had left that she started to talk of the drúkkerébema and the slow start to my magic began. A drúkkerébema, once issued, just has to be fulfilled.

10

'Things you can't begin to understand'

'I don't need to wear that horrid old stifle coat! I won't catch cold! My mam says fresh country air is good for you.'

'This is not fresh country air!'

'It's just blustery. My mam says blustery clears the cobwebs . . . makes you think straight. She says a walk in the wind makes you feel properly well.'

Aunt Emma put on a here-we-go-again expression. 'Freya, you will do exactly as you are told,' she hissed.

I scowled. She was quite running out of patience, but I had to stir her up just a little bit more. My mam doesn't call me trouble with a big T for nothing.

'My mam is the best. My mam knows what's good for me.'

'Just because I don't have children of my own, Freya, doesn't mean that I don't know how to care for you! Now, *please*, put on that coat.'

'*You* are trying too hard. That's the trouble with you fostering folk. You run scared if us little people do anything but breathe.'

'Freya! That's not fair.'

'You've never cared for a proper Romany! You don't understand my mind-thinks. You couldn't possibly love me like my mam!'

Aunt Emma. Nice quiet Aunt Emma suddenly all boiled over.

'But your *perfect* mother just *vanished*, Freya! Your wonderful mother just *dumped* you, with a label round your neck like a *dog*, and left. What do you say about *that*? Do you think that *that* is the correct behaviour for the most sainted mother on earth?'

Aunt Emma was red in the face from crossness. I felt mixed-up-stewed trembly. My mam *had* left me labelled like a dog, but for a very good reason. I knew why. *I knew exactly why*, but I wasn't allowed to tell.

I couldn't let on, for spoiling the magic. The special magic that my mam and my great-gran had entrusted me to do. A drúkkerébema had been issued. Aunt Emma's destiny lay in my hands.

I said nothing but I was quite burned out from crossness and so, judging by her ashen face, was Aunt Emma.

I think she was more angry with herself because she had lost her temper than because I cheeked her. I didn't care. I was upset too.

'She didn't just vanish,' I said, keeping my voice level. 'How many times must I tell you? Someone wanted her urgently, for something important. She had *things* to do.'

'What things?'

I tried not to look shifty-eyed. My mam had told me how town folk didn't understand the importance of the old Romany ways, even Aunt Sally, who should know better. 'Oh I don't know . . . things, things you can't begin to understand.'

'She's left you before.' Aunt Emma sounded calmer now, but more persistent. Downright nosy, in fact. 'You must get upset, feel hurt, to be just abandoned.'

'She comes back! Always she comes back!' I struggled to keep my mixed-up emotions out of my voice.

Aunt Emma nodded sympathetically. 'Freya, I am *sorry*. I *really* am sorry. I should never have lost my temper like that.'

'Me neither,' I admitted. 'My mam says I gets attacks of crossness far too quick . . . like Maggie-Magpie. She says I can be a real grissy-grump if I have a mind to be.'

Aunt Emma smiled. She studied me carefully. I knew what she was really at. She was trying to tell how disturbed I was, because my mam had gone. I didn't need her to worry and fret. I didn't . . . well, not much anyway. We didn't blab, not to outsiders. My great-gran always says we have to learn to stand alone. It gives us strength of character and that is what you need in life.

'I feel fine, thank you very much, Aunt Emma. You'll find no sign of missing screws in me. I can cope for a few short moons, without standing close to my mam.'

I skipped beside her, wearing a smile as bright as my pink flash shoes. I'd show her I hadn't a care in the world. I'd show her.

'Freya,' Aunt Emma said carefully. 'You don't

have to be brave with me. I do understand. It's only natural for a child to miss her mother. It's a *very* disturbing experience.'

'My mam says everything in life is an experience,' I told her firmly, 'and she will come back and everything will be good again soon.'

Aunt Emma took my hand, not to stop me running away, but to show that she really cared. 'Why does she go?' she asked gently.

I snatched my hand back. I didn't want her knowing that I really did miss my mam. If she was any kinder, then I would be sure to cry. I couldn't bear that she should think me soft or something. 'Oh! I 'spect someone wants a baby,' I said, blabbing before I could think straight.

'You're telling me she can make people pregnant? Oh, Freya! Such faith you have in your mam! I've had doctors try and get me pregnant for years. It doesn't happen like that. Just wishing isn't enough, my sweet.'

She was wrong! It was possible, it was, I knew that. I was learning how to help my mam and my great-gran grant wishes. You had to want something really badly, so badly that you hurt deep down inside, and you had to give something back in return, money, or help or just plain love. Nothing is for free, my mam says. We all have to earn a living somehow. I decided Aunt Emma would only think I was talking mumbo-jumbo if I tried to explain, so I changed the subject.

'Well, maybe it's a wedding, something like that.'

I know that I sounded defensive. I was getting more than a teeny bit cross. Mrs Hemmingway,

Aunt Emma to the world's lost lambs, was beginning to ask too many questions. Grown-ups are like that. They ask questions, but they take no notice of your answers. They always think they know best. They think you're talking nonsense, especially when the methods used are those they can't begin to understand.

I am a Romany. Born and bred to the ways of the natural wild. How can I even expect to find a gorgio who can get to grips with the likes of me.

So, I had to really lip-button this time. I knew why my mam left me. I understood why I had to arrive with a label round my neck, all dog-like. There were *details* that I hadn't been told. My mam says that I still blab too much but, if I do my first magic properly, she will tell me more, but I don't think she needs to.

I guess, well, actually I am fairly sure, that the reason for the magic is connected to the night when I saw the grown-ups chatting to a poshrat, a special didakai who was no stranger.

Late that night, when they supposed that I was exhausted from the dance and curled up fast asleep, when I lay, tucked up safe under the vardo with Sabre, Fusty and Woodpile, a lot of whisper words were spoken. That night, my mam had spent hours mulling over old times with Poshrat George. A man who seemed to know almost everything about Aunt Sally. Since then I have had to sew up my lip real tight, so as not to blabber-mouth out the things I heard. Whisper they might, but my ears are bat-wave tuned! It's hard to get a whisper past me!

'I expect the lady lives a long way away and my mam had to go. She's thinking that maybe I should go to school, now I'm big. That's why she left me and, before that, I was too little to take. I'd have gotten in the way.'

'She could stay with you,' Aunt Emma was trying to understand. She, who would half mother-hen a child to death if given a chance, couldn't imagine a reason why Mam should let me be.

'Instead of staying, she just ups and leaves, just to do something for other people. What exactly does she do that's more important to her than you are, Freya?'

'Things you wouldn't understand.'

In my mind, I could see Mam clear as day, gathering herbs in fields and woods, showing me how to choose them at just the right time and pick them in just the right way.

'Sometimes they pays her,' I said, knowing that that wasn't the question that Aunt Emma wanted to ask. 'Sometimes she just does it to help someone. It depends. We Romanies stick together. Even with them who marry gorgios. I expect that someone needed more help from her than me.'

'Well, your mother appears to be quite a character,' Aunt Emma said. She didn't sound as if she liked her very much. 'I'd never leave a child of mine, not with total strangers.'

'You don't understand! She *has* to go. Just like I shall have to go, when I am big. It's even more important that I should go when I am grown because, by then, I shall be able to do even more curing things.'

102

'Why?'

'I told you! I'm a chime child.'

Aunt Emma didn't ask me to explain, so I didn't bother to try. I didn't know it all yet. My mam says that I still have a lot of learning to do. That's why she's pondering about me trying school for a while. She's *sometimes* keen, even if I'm not.

My mam is tough. What she says goes. She had a difficult life growing up with a dibby mam. My great-gran helped all she could, but things were very hard for her. She's still not over sure that school is best for me.

Aunt Emma let the label thing drop and I was grateful. Everything was peaceful. Well, right up until the early evening when I went and spoiled things *again*.

That evening I made a big mistake. I really succeeded in spooking Aunt Emma *and* Uncle Jack. I tried bringing baby bird down to have supper with us. Aunt Emma was not amused.

Uncle Jack was. I could see him trying not to laugh, but he didn't stop Aunt Emma from going more than a little mad. They have to gang up together, grown-ups, don't they? I wish I knew why!

'Can't you keep that wretched thing in the shed! Haven't you any idea how unhygienic it is to have a bird sharing a meal with you?'

'It was lonely! Why can't it share with us?'

'Aunt Emma's right, darling. One doesn't usually have a bird at the table. They do carry an awful lot of germs. You don't let dogs into your wagons,

103

do you?' Uncle Jack was using his let's-be-reasonable-darling voice. I ignored it.

'You folks lets dogs in your houses.'

'Exactly!' Uncle Jack said triumphantly. '*Some* people let dogs share their houses. They're less hygienic than you gypsies in that respect. But even they don't share their table with birds.'

'It's a baby. You're s'posed to like babies!' I summoned up real salty tears and let them drip down my nose. 'How can you have me here, when you don't like children?'

'That's a cruel gibe, Freya!' Uncle Jack stood up to show me how angry he was. 'Poor Aunt Emma and I have spent years trying to have a baby. We've . . .'

'Jack, don't! It's not necessary.'

'It most certainly is. This spoilt little gypsy brat is going to learn that I won't have you upset.' He turned towards me, his face a mixture of sadness and anger.

'We've tried everything! Times, temperatures, hospitals, operations. Things that you would never believe possible. If Aunt Emma and I don't have a baby, then you can believe me that it's not through lack of trying. So don't you ever try a stunt like that again, Freya Boswell, or I'll dump you back in your lovely muddy fields and you can wait for your sainted mother there!'

'Jack!'

'Jack, nothing! Now stop that snivelling, girl. If you want to discuss something, do it properly. Don't revel in other people's weaknesses. It is not in the least becoming!'

Uncle Jack sat down. I looked down at my shoes and for a long time nobody said anything. Aunt Emma pretended to eat her supper and Uncle Jack just folded his arms and waited. Never ever had I seen him so wound-up cross.

'Maggie has to live in the warm,' I said. 'She can't live in the shed.'

'Well, she certainly isn't living at the table,' Uncle Jack said firmly. 'Not in this house!'

'Can I still keep her in my room?' I said, my voice pleading, but with no tears. Maggie and I were glue-stuck friends. If she went, then I would go with her.

'How about that magic word *please*?'

'*Please*, if I keep my room really clean. No specks of dust anywhere. Please can I keep her in my nice warm room? And I'm sorry if I upset you. I never realised that you hurt so deep about babies. Not so very deep inside.'

Aunt Emma and Uncle Jack drew shutters round their faces. They obviously thought that they had let me see too deep in their hearts.

'To keep the room clean you will have to use lots and lots of elbow grease.'

'Can we buy some tomorrow?'

Aunt Emma looked at Uncle Jack. Uncle Jack looked at Aunt Emma and they both burst out laughing. I stared at them gobsmacked. One minute they were spitting-blood cross, the next they were laughing. They were more Romany moody than me!

'Elbow grease is pure hard work, Freya,' Aunt

Emma explained. 'It means dusting and polishing *every single day.*'

'So, if that bird shits, *you* clean it up, not Aunt Emma.'

I stared at Uncle Jack. He had deliberately used that word to shock me. I kept my face deadpan flat. I didn't let on that, in my tribe, words like that are used *all* the time.

'The bird can't help it, Uncle Jack. It's only little, but I'll use lots of elbow grease, I promise. Just let me keep her in my room.'

'*Please.*'

'Please.'

Uncle Jack and Aunt Emma nodded at the same time. I wanted to laugh but I didn't. My head was full of a mixture of mixed-up feelings. They weren't bad really. It *was* a smelly bird and, if I was honest, I was a far cry from the pretty baby in a frill-flounced crib that they obviously spent so much time dreaming of.

They were hurting real bad inside. Every time they saw a baby, they hid lost-hope tears. My mam and my great-gran did magic for people like them and now they were teaching me. I have special powers. I can help when things are *really* difficult. One day soon, I shall be the greatest choviar.

'Chime, now is the time for you to work alone,' they had told me and all because my mam met a long-lost kinsman, one who'd told her all about a mother hen called Sally.

11

'Grown-ups always cause trouble'

'It was such a lovely tea party,' Aunt Emma said, picking up her duster. I certainly enjoyed it. I think it went really well.'

My mouth fish-faced gaped. I had forgotten the silly party days ago.

'Did it truly make you feel happy-heart good?'

Aunt Emma polished even harder, as if she was scrubbing her happy memories deep into her head.

'We had such a pleasant conversation. Mrs Plumpton is really quite interesting and the Reverend Plumpton was quite impressed with the garden. He says the vicarage garden has been neglected for far too long. Freya, he has such exciting plans, both for the church and for the land.'

I stared at her, eye-gaze straight. There was not a hint of her teasing voice. She actually *was* pleased, so pleased that she was still feeling mind-hippy-happy after three whole days.

'What was the best bit?' I asked, poky-nose curious.

Aunt Emma stopped polishing and shrugged. 'Oh, I don't know, it was so English, so traditional.

What could be nicer than a quiet cup of tea on your own lawn with friends?'

'Uncle Jack said the Plumptons were acquaintances.'

'You can't hurry things too much, Freya. Mrs Plumpton is meeting so many new people, but I am sure we will end up good friends, given a little time.'

I felt sorry for Aunt Emma. She had so many empty hours to fill. She took in children like me, but it wasn't enough. She hated the thought of long empty spaces.

'What's gorgio traditional? Tell me some more things.'

'Tea on the lawn, Sunday church, bacon and eggs for breakfast,' Aunt Emma's face grew painful-line drawn, 'singing nursery rhymes to your children.'

'They'd mess up your ever so neat lawn,' I said, wearing *my* best teasing voice. She was losing her hippy-happies and becoming far too sad.

Aunt Emma gave me a watery smile. I tried again.

'We have singing and talking and campfires . . . and vardo burning.' It was *my* turn to look glum. When my great-gran dies, she'll burn her vardo and that's the very last thing that I want her to do.

I sighed. My chitter chatter with Aunt Emma had not gone well at all. She was left sad and so was I. I retreated to the wild garden and left her to scrub away her sadness with a lemon-scented get-up-your-nose polish spray.

My great-gran says that if a day starts badly, it can only get worse, so you may as well forget it. I had broken Aunt Emma's happy mind-thinks and because of *that*, she went mad with her polish.

Grown-ups always cause trouble. They can never leave things just as they should be. My room wasn't that bad! I could live in it. She said that if I used elbow grease she wouldn't interfere.

I thought Maggie would be safe with the window open. Like me, Maggie wanted to feel free, not shut up, in case she needed to go. It would've been all right, but I forgot all about Aunt Emma's belief that the room should for ever be sprayed and have nice clean sheets.

Aunt Emma must have opened my bedroom door and sniffed. It smelled of hot stale bird. Bird smell is stinky strong. Feathered folk are supposed to live in nests, where the smell doesn't matter. They weren't designed to be strutting round bed-rooms. I did my best to hide the odour of strong smelly bird, but I never managed to do it right.

Tincture of Maggie was stale and funny. It made the room smell pungent, even though I elbow-greased away for hours and hours to try and please Aunt Emma. I used cloths and perfumed detergents until I thought both Maggie and I would drown in a sea of funny scents, but it made no difference whatsoever. The room smelled of magpie and that was that.

While I was in the garden, Aunt Emma must have gone into my room to polish and change the sheets. She must've pulled the big sheets straight off the bed and scared Maggie half to death.

I was so cross that I couldn't even think straight when Aunt Emma came tearing down the stairs, her face as white as a sheet, shouting, 'Maggie's gone! She flew straight out of the window!'

I just stared at her, all wordless.

'Freya, Maggie's gone! Oh, Freya, I'm so sorry. I know how you love that bird.'

'She's too young to mind herself!' I raised my fists to thump Aunt Emma. Bossy house-proud madam that she was. I raised my fists in right royal anger and I was just about to strike her when I saw that her face was filled with proper tears. My hands dropped, and needing to see to believe, I followed her indoors.

Nobody had ever cried when I had lost a pet before. My mam would make me cake and build a little cross, but she never cried, not even when our great old horse Geddie broke his leg and had to be shot. Not even when she held his rein as Papa blew out his brains to stop him paining so much. Not even then. The only time she ever cried was when she said goodbye to Pansy.

'Don't matter!' I hefted the window open, so as the room didn't stink so much to remind me. 'It's my fault too. I'll just go and have a quick look for her anyhow. If her hungry tum is hopeful, well then, she might stay close.'

'She may have flown too far,' Aunt Emma warned me, her voice sweet-breeze gentle as we went back out to search the garden.

I put on a brave face. Just like my mam did when Geddie died. 'Her flying feathers are nearly grown. Perhaps she will be fine without me.' I let myself into the garden. '*Maggie! Maggie!*'

There was no sign of my precious little chíniko

friend anywhere. No answering chatter, no matter how often I called.

'*Maggie! Maggie!*'

There was no sound, just echo-back silence.

I headed off down to the secret garden and still there was no clue. I sat myself down, on the small stone seat at the side of the pond, and wiped away the tears that were falling down my face in buckets, even if a gypsy chavi should never cry. 'Pansy, if you are here in this special place, please help me find my little bird,' I sobbed, sinking deep into a thick soup of misery.

Nothing moved. Nothing moved, except Aunt Emma who had come to find me.

'It *really was* an accident, Freya. I was only changing sheets. You must believe me.'

I nodded. 'I know it was an accident. It could've happened to anybody. It's not important,' I said, but both she and I were well aware that it was.

'Maggie!' called out Aunt Emma, more to show how she was trying than in hope. We both listened, but the only thing to be heard was the faint rustling of wind-tossed leaves.

'*Maggie!*' I shouted, to show Aunt Emma that I was joining in and not wallowing in being sad. Again we stopped and listened. Again and again and again.

Hoarse with calling, Aunt Emma and I stopped trying. We just sat in the garden, wondering what to do next. Suddenly, halfway up the big yew on the side edge next to our garden, came a magpie squawk. 'It's Maggie!' I called to Aunt Emma. '*It really is Maggie!*'

111

I held out my hand and spoke her name again, but Maggie only squawked. She'd been properly spooked and was too scared to leave the safety of the great old tree.

'I'll go and get a ladder,' Aunt Emma whispered. 'You just keep calling softly and maybe she'll come to you. If she doesn't, then you distract her and I'll climb up the tree and grab her.'

I called and called, but Maggie-Magpie only watched me. She didn't even squawk back.

After what seemed like ages, Aunt Emma staggered towards me, dragging a great big ladder that she'd fetched from the garage.

'I'll climb,' I said. 'I've got younger feet.'

'No! You've already been lost. What do you think your social worker would say, if you slipped and broke your leg? She wouldn't say, "Well done, Mrs Hemmingway," that's for sure.'

Aunt Emma struggled to position the ladder against the trunk of the ancient yew so that it didn't wobble too much. 'I wish Jack was here,' she muttered. 'He's far better than me at things like this.' She shook the ladder a bit to test for its safeness. All the time, Maggie watched her and I watched Maggie.

'He's the one,' Aunt Emma continued in a low voice, chatting more to herself than to me, 'that prunes this great overgrown old yew, when it hangs too far over the fence. Even Jack though says he'll only trim it again when he is really sure that Mrs Plumpton is safely shut up in the church.'

'Why?'

'Well, for one thing, we don't want to upset the

112

Plumptons. We are, after all, hoping to be friends and, for another, he's not sure it's right to prune even an ugly yew when it's on church property.'

'It's not ugly . . . just churchy. Yews are preaching-proper in churches, aren't they?'

'Well, they're not *proper*, overhanging my garden,' Aunt Emma said starchily, as she leaned the ladder very carefully against the great yew that bounded the corner of our garden.

Maggie didn't move. She just watched Aunt Emma, as if it was the most natural thing in the world to have a ladder trying to push you out of your tree.

Aunt Emma hitched up her skirt so as she could climb up the ladder. I held the bottom as steady as I could by standing on the bottom rung. Maggie watched us with bright beady eyes, but still she didn't move. She acted as if she was pasty glue stuck to the branch of the tree.

Very slowly, Aunt Emma climbed up the steps. I was impressed. I would've rushed up and been far too hasty. I'd have probably frightened Maggie away.

When she was just in reach, Aunt Emma held out her hand. I really thought she'd made it but she hadn't. Maggie just hopped straight out of her reach, as if she was playing catcher-catch-me.

Over in the vicarage garden I heard rustling. I guessed Mrs Plumpton was sipping tea and reading a book in the afternoon sunshine. I hoped that she wasn't too cross with us for disturbing her churchyard yew.

Aunt Emma was marvellous. She didn't do any

more than whisper, 'Blast!' under her breath, before she tried to catch Maggie again. Maggie-Magpie thought this was great fun and hopped even further up the great gnarled yew. 'Blast you, stupid bird!' Aunt Emma said, just a little louder, and I didn't dare warn her that the rustling on the other side of the fence was growing louder too.

Aunt Emma pulled the ladder away from the fence, opened it up to its very longest and propped it back against the trunk of the tree. Again she climbed very slowly and suddenly it occurred to me that, not only was she trying not to scare Maggie, but she was more than a little bit frightened of heights too.

'Come down, pretty boy! Come down, you stupid little bugger,' Aunt Emma sang softly as she reached out for Maggie again. I held on to the bottom of the trembling ladder and began to worry myself about whether we were doing the right thing.

Maybe it *was* time for Maggie to be free. She didn't seem too keen to be back in our nice warm house. Perhaps my Kackaratchi-Kackaratchi longed for big wild fields and scrubby woods like I did. Her feathers were being soft-wind blown and her head was probably being filled with the scent of spring-sweet resins.

'Give up, Aunt Emma! Please come down. She's almost properly feathered. Even her end feathers are tough-tail tall,' I called to Aunt Emma, but already it was too late.

In that instant, Aunt Emma lunged towards Maggie and, just as she had her safe in her hand, she lost her footing. Maggie fluttered out of Aunt Emma's hand, that opened as she unbalanced, in a desperate bid to catch hold of some branches. Maggie, minus a tail feather, flew right to the top of the ancient yew.

After that, for what seemed like ages, nothing moved. Aunt Emma stood on the very top of her tippy toes, on the highest rung of the real tall ladder, her hands outstretched as if in prayer. Maggie-Magpie peered down at her from the trembling top of the great yew. It seemed as if she was finding our rescue tries really funny.

I stood, gum-stuck rigid, at the bottom of the ladder, desperately hoping that Aunt Emma would manage to make herself stable. Then, all at once, it happened. Branches snapped and little bits of dust and yew blew out, like well-kicked puffballs. Aunt Emma slipped, shrieked and moaned. All the time more branches broke and more bits of twig and dust flew into the air. I watched, mouth-buttoned thunderstruck.

After what seemed like for ever, Aunt Emma hit the ground. The ghostly silence that followed roared loud in my ears.

I rushed over, as fast as I could, even though my legs felt all crumbly with scaredness. Aunt Emma had landed in a tangled heap right at the bottom of that stupid great yew. Luckily, she was on our side of the fence and cushioned a bit by the compost heap. I was ever so glad it was dry. I bent over and gently touched her head. While I was trying to stroke her into wakefulness, she opened her eyes.

'*STUPID, STUPID BLOODY BIRD!*' she shouted, more in fright than in anger. '*STUPID, STUPID BLOODY BIRD!*'

A snort of muffled laughter rose like a wakening mist from the other side of the vicarage fence. Aunt Emma pulled down her skirt and her face was as white as the nice fresh sheets that had caused her so much trouble.

'Mrs *Plumpton*!' we both whispered in unison.

'I'll never dare speak to her again,' Aunt Emma told me, forgetting to whisper. 'She'll never want to be my friend now, not after I've used such very rude words.'

I felt guilty. Aunt Emma had only been trying to help me and now she had, most likely, upset her snobby old neighbours.

Maggie was still at the top of the tree, watching us with bright beady eyes, but we had lost heart. We brushed each other down and got ready to carry the ladder back to its proper place in the garage.

The top of Mrs Plumpton's head appeared over the fence. She was red-faced with laughter. 'Oh, Mrs Hemmingway!' she said. 'Please don't worry yourself about a few rude words. The conditions you were under, I think that I would have used words that were far, far more explicit than that.'

Aunt Emma and I stared at the vicar's wife, our mouths opened wide in amazement.

'My dears, you have given me a really wonderful afternoon's entertainment. I haven't enjoyed myself so much in years.'

Aunt Emma and I said nothing. Mrs Plumpton

116

stood on the very tips of her toes so that even more of her grinning face showed.

'Oh, being a vicar's wife can be so boring, my dears. Everyone expects you to behave like a perfect saint, and it's just not possible. Life's not like that at all, is it? No, it's not! But it has to be for the vicar's wife and it's just not fair.'

Aunt Emma began to smile. The smile turned into a grin. The grin dissolved into giggles. The two grown women were standing either side of the fence, hooting with laughter. I couldn't quite see what was so very funny.

I was forgotten. I took my chance to have a last quiet word with Maggie.

'Keep yourself safe, Kackaratchi-Kackaratchi. Grow big and strong and just sometimes, when you're not specially busy, well, just sometimes remember me.'

Maggie blinked as if she understood that I was trying to say goodbye. Although I felt sad now, I knew that, soon, she would just be a happy memory; rather like my baby sister Pansy, who had seemed to smile when my mam let me give her a last goodbye cuddle.

Now, at long last, I knew what my great-gran was telling me, when she had insisted that mementoes were not really important. Saying that only soft modern Romanies, like my mam, used them. They just made the letting go of a loved one a little bit easier.

Maggie would never totally disappear. After all, I only had to think of Pansy. Her memory had not faded, not even after all this time. That was because a tiny bit of Pansy was, somehow, locked in my heart for ever.

12

'Aunt Emma thought I was telling porky pies again'

'Now, are you going to wear your nice new trainers when we visit Sally and her family? You did say that you liked them. Have you a decent coat, Freya? Just in case it turns cold again. Perhaps you would let me buy you a new one. That one does look a bit as if it's seen better days.'

I knew that she was trying to make me forget about losing my baby magpie. I guessed that she was trying to keep me occupied. I didn't want to be *occupied*. I wanted to be able to think my sad thoughts, over and over, so that one day I could remember the good times. I thought about my baby sister having her one and only bath after birthing and I thought about my magpie having such fun in hers.

'Penny for your thoughts?'

She was interrupting again. She didn't understand that it was OK to be sometimes sad. Angry at being interrupted, I attacked.

'You're a bit cross that that posh Sally's got seven kids and you haven't got any, aren't you?' I said before I could remember the trouble that winding her up about babies had got me into before.

It wasn't that I really wanted to hurt her. I just wanted to avoid the embarrassing question of whether I wanted a scratchy new coat. I didn't want to admit that the comfy tatty coat that I clung to was the only one that I had ever had.

'Don't be silly, Freya! Sally is my very best friend,' Aunt Emma retorted, and her voice was cross, her lips set thin, and her spine maypole-rigid, making me quite proud of the way I'd appeared so calm when she'd needled me about silly coats and shoes.

'And, anyway, I told you the seventh isn't even due to be born yet.'

'And I'm telling you that the baby *is* born and they're going to call him James. James is a gorgio grand name, don't you think?'

Aunt Emma thought that I was telling porky pies again, I could tell. She waited for me to talk about something else but I didn't, so we ate the rest of our meal in silence.

She couldn't bring herself to ask how I was so very sure that the baby had been born. Even a gorgio would have known what she was thinking about. Aunt Emma said we were quiet because we'd used up all our energy earlier in the garden, but I knew that was a lie. I might have spent my time running free but I'm not stupid. She was half frightened to go and find out if I was really right. She loved her friend Sally dearly but was a green-eyed envy cat when it came to the baby.

I can tell, by the time and sense of things, events

that she won't ever guess and I'd succeeded in needling her into more than half believing. She was in a hurry to leave the table. Nosiness was growing in her mind. It wasn't polite, to go and telephone halfway through a meal. I wasn't allowed to leave the table until all of us were finished, and so neither could she, even though she was dying with curiousness.

She couldn't *wait* to telephone Sally to see if her silly baby really was born. The moment we were finished, she cleared away and rushed to the phone. She dialled the number and listened with bated breath.

I sat on the bottom stair by the telephone, watching her carefully. I was trying not to laugh and she knew. She threw me a look that meant it's-about-time-that-you-grew-up! I stuffed my fist in my mouth so I wouldn't giggle aloud and be sent away.

'Hello, Sally? . . . Oh!'

There was a long pause and then, 'Oh dear! Three pounds two ounces, you say? Well, that's not too small these days, is it?' There was another long pause then, 'Prem. babies are often poorly at first, especially the first few days . . .'

I nudged Aunt Emma. 'Tell her to tell Sally not to worry. Tell her James will be all right, really he will. Aunt Emma, TELL HER PLEASE!'

Aunt Emma frowned at me and then, pressing the silence switch, she said, 'Well, it is a comforting thought, so I will.' She did as I asked, obviously feeling more than a little foolish.

'My new foster-child, Freya. Somehow she knew

the baby was born. She's adamant that the baby will be fine. She says to tell you that James will get better very soon.'

I smiled. Aunt Emma wasn't at all bad really. She did listen to me after all. Not many grown-ups would have even pretended to believe me. Poor Aunt Emma, who was so jealous really, and all because she couldn't seem to get a baby of her own.

'How on earth did Freya guess the baby's name is James? It was only decided to call him James today. So the poor little mite could be christened . . . just in case . . .'

The voice on the other end of the line was so shocked and loud I could hear it myself, even though I was now on the third stair up.

'I don't know. Freya insists that you are not to worry. She has some funny little ways but she's rather charming. She says not to fret at all. She says the baby will turn out to be the usual sort of horrid little boy. As you can see, Freya doesn't put babies very high on her list of preferences.'

They chatted some more before Aunt Emma replaced the receiver. I disappeared the moment that I was sure that my message had been relayed. Aunt Emma had spoken well of me, even if I was so often rude to her.

It was in that moment that the power of the drúkkerébema flowed through me, just as my great-gran had promised it would. Now I had no choice. My heart would be flitter-flutter filled until the parsley was properly planted. Parsley is an uncanny herb; for me it will work wonderful magic. I am a chime child. If parsley is the lock then I am the key. All I needed now, was for Uncle Jack to remember to buy me the seeds.

But magic went straight out of my mind as soon as I heard that dreadful squawk. Aunt Emma and I rushed to the window. I pointed to the flurry of fighting feathers in the middle of the garden. A whole bunch of starlings was attacking something and I knew instantly that it was Maggie-Magpie.

'Why?' Aunt Emma asked, her face almost as white as mine.

'She smells human,' I explained. 'Oh, Aunt Emma, what on earth are we going to do?'

We raced to the door and the starlings fled. Poor Maggie-Magpie tried to flee as well, but she was too battered and too bruised and even more of her flying feathers were missing. She attempted to fly down the garden, but she lost height, like a dying war plane, and fell, slap bang, into the middle of the wild-garden pond.

Aunt Emma and I looked at each other. After what seemed like an eternity, Aunt Emma nodded. 'Take off your shoes, Freya. The pond's quite deep in the middle, so be very careful indeed not to slip.'

I pulled off my shoes and socks in no time at all and waded into the pond. The water was cold and I nearly lost my balance and skidded off one of the outer pond ledges, despite all Aunt Emma's warnings. I thought I did really well to balance back upright.

Maggie had stopped her desperate splashing and

was lying quite still. Just a little bundle of blacky blue and white feathers, with not a single squawk.

It was very deep in the middle. I'd pulled up my skirt and tucked it in my knickers, but still I got soaked right up to my middle. I could only move slowly and I was blue-pimple cold. Aunt Emma was already taking off her shoes and tucking up her skirt, so that she would be ready to rescue me if I fell.

Maggie-Magpie didn't do anything when I scooped her up. I was ever so careful, but she didn't blink or even open her eyes to show that she knew she was safe. She didn't do anything at all.

Tears streamed down my face, as I carried her back to Aunt Emma. I didn't mind that I was wet and cold and dirty. I only cared that the little magpie, that I loved so much, was just a bundle of wet and manky feathers. It was a rotten way to die, chased out by almost your own kind. It happens to gypsies all the time, mainly because we get mixed up with New Age travellers, but at least we don't get killed for being different. Though my great-gran says that we were sometimes murdered in olden times, especially in times of war.

'It's dead!' I told Aunt Emma sadly. 'I was too late and she's dead.'

Aunt Emma gently took Maggie-Magpie's tiny body out of my hands and examined her carefully. Then she looked long and hard at me.

I stood, pond-muddy and miserable, with tears pouring, but I could not think of a word to say.

Nothing came into my head, except that it was time for the cross and prayer bit.

To my surprise, Aunt Emma started blowing gently into the little nose holes at the top of Magpie's beak. At the same time she rubbed its soggy wet chest with her thumb. Every now and then she turned the magpie over and shook her gently, dislodging tiny drops of muddy water.

I watched every move she made, quite forgetting to be goosepimple cold. I was just about to think that it was a complete waste of time, all that blowing and stroking, when my baby bird spluttered and sneezed!

'It's still very poorly,' Aunt Emma warned me as we raced indoors forgetting to wipe feet and everything. 'I know! Brandy and a hairdryer, that will warm it up.' She sent me upstairs for a hairdryer while she searched for brandy, all the time clutching the wet little bundle of feathers that was supposed to be Maggie.

'How much brandy?'

'To be honest, Freya, I haven't a clue, but she does need something to warm her up fast. We shall just have to take a chance. Is that all right with you?'

I nodded. Aunt Emma put a few drops of brandy into a glass and added a sprinkle of sugar and a little water. While she did that, I warmed my magpie gently with the hairdryer, being careful to use the lowest setting and not to hold it too close.

Maggie moved a little bit and her feathers got fluffed, but she never looked beady-eyed and her eyes were near-dead dull.

Aunt Emma gently took Maggie-Magpie away from me and tilted her head. 'Drop the brandy down her beak, like you did with the honey water the day you found her.'

I tried but Maggie didn't splutter, she just lay there, as limp as wilted cabbage.

'Try dropping it over her nostrils. She'll have to swallow to breathe.'

I did as I was told, but again nothing happened. The brandy seeped away but Maggie didn't move.

'Oh well! If in doubt, try brute force,' Aunt Emma muttered and grasped the little magpie's head with one hand as it rested on her lap and slid one of her nice long nails along the side of its beak, until she found a place where she could lever it partly open. 'Try now!'

I dropped some more brandy water straight on to her tongue. Maggie-Magpie spluttered and coughed. Some of the brandy had definitely gone down her throat this time.

Maggie opened her eyes and coughed again. Already, the look in her eye was a little brighter. Aunt Emma and I felt safe enough to glance at each other and smile.

As Maggie-Magpie slowly began to feel warm from her inside out, I began to feel frozen to my very skin. It was only now that I realised that I was full of shiveriness.

'Hot bath!' Aunt Emma ordered. 'At once.'

'But Maggie needs me.'

'No, she doesn't. You have a bath. I'll give Maggie one more sip of brandy and then I'll tuck her up in her nice warm tissue-paper bed for a much-needed sleep. You can check she's OK before you go to bed too.'

Aunt Emma sorted out Magpie as best she could and then came up to make sure that I was warm and clean and dry.

'Can I have some brandy too?'

'I don't think you'll like it.'

'Please! I got wet as well, didn't I?'

'You were a big brave girl. I was really proud of you,' Aunt Emma said and she let me have a spoonful of brandy, with no sugar water at all, as I had got cold and wet too. It was awful! I spat it out because it burned my tongue and Aunt Emma laughed. 'Teach you to I-want!' she said.

When I woke up in the morning, Maggie was wide awake, alive and squawking.

'Maggie, ssh!'

Squawk, squawk.

'Maggie, shut your gob!'

'Squawk, *squawk*!

'Maggie, yesterday Aunt Emma and I went to a great deal of trouble to save your stupid little life. *Now shut up!*'

SQUAWK, SQUAWK, SQUAWK!

She was drunk as a lord, she was! Three in the morning, long before cock-crow and she was busy squawking her little heart out. It was impossible to sleep. I imagined that Mrs Plumpton could hear her, even on the other side of that great church yew. I bet that, even after all that giggling, she wouldn't be too impressed, not with us having a more-than-half-cut motto bird.

Just as I expected, Uncle Jack and Aunt Emma appeared, bleary-eyed, at my bedroom door.

'Can't you shut that bird up? I've got to go to work today!' Uncle Jack moaned.

Squawk, squawk, flutter, flutter, *squawk*, Maggie-Magpie replied, and tried to climb out of her cardboard-box nest to greet them and the not-nearly-close morning.

She perched on the edge, waving about with no control at all, before falling back inside, still wing-flapping and chattering madly.

'Freya, *explain*! What have you done to it?'

'Nothing,' I said, worried that Aunt Emma might get told off, if I let on about using his very best brandy. 'Nothing at all.'

Aunt Emma fidgeted with the cords of her long white dressing-gown. 'Come on, Jack! It's not her fault that the bird is singing, is it?'

'Your bird is not singing! Good God, child, even a zombie can tell that. It's raving drunk!'

I drew my blankets up round my chin and tried to look nonchalant. 'It looks OK to me.'

'Well, from where I'm standing, it looks drunk as a skunk! What magpie do you know that lies upside down in a cardboard box, waving its feet in the air and singing?'

We gave in. Neither of us had ever seen a magpie upside-down happy and squawking in delight ... not ever.

'It's drunk,' Aunt Emma and I admitted in unison.

'How?' Uncle Jack asked, happy now that he was not being fobbed off.

'I was going to tell you, but you were so tired when you eventually came home that I decided it could wait until morning.'

'What could?'

Uncle Jack was wide awake and curious now. He seemed better able to ignore Magpie's pathetic attempts to sing. He sat down on the edge of my bed with Aunt Emma and waited.

'Aunt Emma saved Maggie's life last night, but to do it, she had to use some of your very best brandy.'

'Freya was very brave yesterday. She waded into the pond and, despite being cold and wet, she rescued her little pet magpie.'

Uncle Jack grinned at us both. 'Well, as we seem to have such an obvious mutual admiration society, I think that you should tell me every single thing about it.'

So we did and Uncle Jack listened to every word and didn't mind any more that his very best brandy had been used . . . or that I tasted some too . . . and thought it was really quite horrid.

13

'Freya, I've warned you before about not hurting people'

Aunt Emma came to find me. Unfortunately, I was sitting in the garden with my feet in the goldfish pond. My feet felt ever so hot after wearing my flashy shoes, even though they were painted in happy colours. I expected her to go mad when she saw me, but she stayed smiling.

Maggie-Magpie, none the worse for her adventure, was rooting round in the grass, trying to catch insects and worms all by herself.

'You're not interested in babies, are you?' Aunt Emma teased, stepping carefully over the bird to sit beside me. 'Such a pity, because Sally lives by some lovely fields, and a pretty big copse is there too. I was thinking of taking you with me to see her, but the mere thought of babies and you run away! So I can't see *you* being willing to admire Sally's new baby, can I?'

I pretended to ignore her. She was right. Babies and brothers are a pain in the neck. I have six brothers, all bigger than me, and I had one sister too, but she went and died before she was even two days old. Babies don't bother me any more. Babies are usually trouble.

'You look sad?'

'I was thinking about Pansy.'

'Who's Pansy?'

'Pansy was my little sister. Well, she would've been if she hadn't been born all blue and black because her heart was too poorly to mend.'

'Oh, I'm sorry, Freya.'

'That's why my mam called her Pansy. Blue and black face, she had. My mam had to think of a name to call her real quick.'

Aunt Emma sat down beside me. She didn't talk. She just sat close and waited.

'I loved Pansy. She was real cute, tiny fingers and toeses.' I wiped away the tears that it had never seemed proper to shed before, for fear of upsetting my mam. 'She was wide-eyed wonderful, was Pansy. When she died, they burned her, just as it is proper, in a crematorium like you gorgios. They burned all the little clothes that my mam had made for her, everything. They did it at night when they thought I was sandman sleeping. They even burned the teddy that I bought her. Almost everything was fired to ashes ... except a few things sneaked away by my mam.'

'Why?' Aunt Emma's voice was so soft that I was only just aware that she had spoken.

'I'm not sure. We always burn dead people's things. Everything she has, she should take with her, that's what great-gran says. My mam though is what my great-gran calls a soft modern Romany.

She let *nearly* everything be burned, but kept one small memento for each of us.'

'What did your mam keep?'

'My mam kept the blanket that wrapped her and I kept the posy of flowers I gave her while she was dying. My mam put a new blanket and fresh flowers in her box for her to take with her. That way, she said, Pansy wouldn't mind, even if great-gran made all the fuss in the world. My mam says it's nice to have something to hold, while we learn to say goodbye.'

'I'm sure that Pansy's gone somewhere nice.'

Aunt Emma wasn't certain how I would react to the idea of heaven, I could tell, and anyhow, I wasn't sure about discussing Pansy. Her memory is still tight-tangled deep inside so I pretended not to notice that Aunt Emma was holding my hand.

'I sun-dried Pansy's little flowers. I still have them tucked away, safely hidden in a tin in Great-gran's vardo. Her failing white eyes won't ever spot them there.'

Aunt Emma said nothing. She just continued to hold my hand.

'I expect she's in some lovely field,' I said at last, so that the sad thinking should be finished and, all of a sudden, I had an idea, 'or, in a lovely safe wild garden like this. Do you think she could be here, Aunt Emma?'

'Pansy will be wherever your heart is, Freya. I think she could well be by this pond now, being pleased that you love her so and she's not for-gotten.'

I felt happier. I didn't talk. I let go of Aunt

Emma's hand and made myself busy, pulling petals off a daisy one by one. Aunt Emma might be a bit dull at times but she was warm-heart kind.

I started singing 'Shall I? Shan't I?' to a very special tune. It was important not to stop halfway through. When I was quite finished I gave Aunt Emma a giant-sized grin. If she understood that I loved my sister, maybe better than all my brothers who were far bigger than me, she couldn't be all that bad, could she?

My brothers hadn't even taken a keepsake. 'She's not lived proper,' they said gruffly, 'and, anyway, her things is better burned.' I had been angry, but my mam had soothed my crossness. 'They's young men! They have to appear tough with their mates. They can't be seen to be crying over little Pansy who, after all, only just happened. Don't think that they don't care, Freya. That gruffness and rudeness is only buried sadness.'

Aunt Emma still sat all quiet beside me. She had shared my tear-thoughts and earned something happy. I sang my daisy song again. Maggie-Magpie stopped looking for grubs and came and sat on my knee while I sang. She tilted her head on one side, as if she was checking carefully that I had sung the tune exactly right.

'I know what I must do,' I told Aunt Emma when I was finished. I let a grin spread from ear to ear. 'The daisies have quite made up my mind.'

'Tell me!'

I shook my head and laughed. She gave me a really special smile, showing she understood that I could be happy and sad, all in the same moment.

'I'm going inside now, if you don't mind. Be careful of the water, not that I care if you get soaked, but you might damage my lovely pond. Also, Mrs Plumpton would most definitely not be amused to see a protégé of mine in a pond twice in one week.'

I laughed. She was teasing. I had learned her teasing voice. I pulled out my feet, being careful not to damage her pretty pond plants, and followed her indoors. Maggie-Magpie, sensing that I was about to go, scrambled up on to my shoulder.

I thought and thought about how I was going to grant Aunt Emma and Uncle Jack's heart's desire. Even the buying of parsley seeds was not proving as easy as I had thought.

When I'd stood so nervously on their doorstep, with a label round my neck and just a carry bag full of my few belongings, I'd trusted that I would be able to do my magic all alone . . . once that is, I was safely settled.

Now I was wiser. Gorgio folk are miles apart in thinking from us. I would have to have some help. I decided that the best person to ask, now that the time of the drúkkerébema was decided, was Uncle Jack.

It was always difficult, finding a time to talk to Uncle Jack alone. He was a bustle-busy man. I was usually in bed when he came home, but however late it was, he always came to kiss me goodnight. I liked Uncle Jack, right from the very start, even though he sometimes took it into his head to remind me of my manners.

I made up my mind not to be too sleepy to tell

him about my great idea. I lay awake for ages and was almost convinced that he wasn't going to come. My eyes were all but sandman-sleepy stuck, when he crept up to my bed to kiss me goodnight.

'Sorry I was so late, poppet. Crisis at the office.'

I grinned. There was always a crisis at the office. His work was really important to him.

'Is your work more important than a baby?'

Uncle Jack scowled. 'Freya, I've warned you before about not hurting people.'

'I'm not trying to upset you, Uncle Jack. I was only wanting to know if *you* needed a baby as much as Aunt Emma does.'

'A baby would be something to rush home for, Freya. Sometimes I can't bear the sadness on Emma's face when people ask us if we're not thinking of children, or when we have to go and admire the latest new arrival. Yes, I'd love a baby too . . . almost as much as Emma!'

My tummy trembles vanished. The time to be doing was properly marked. I reached out and grasped his hairy hand. 'Uncle Jack, do you think you could listen to what will sound to you like a very silly plan?'

'Believe me, I'm a good listener, Freya. That's how most problems are solved . . . listening.'

'It'll sound soup-head silly, but you really have to help and you have to promise not to tell. It's *very* important not to let on a single word. It's a real sticky-stuck-mouth secret, that I'm going to share with you.'

'I promise,' Uncle Jack said seriously and I wondered how he would feel about that promise when I told him what he was going to have to help me do.

14

'You're sounding very mysterious, Freya'

It was raining. Aunt Emma and I were busy in the kitchen and Maggie-Magpie was banished to the bedroom in the interests of hygiene.

We were making pretty fairy cakes, with bright colour icing, and decorating them with the teeniest teeniest silver balls that I had ever seen. I felt close to Aunt Emma, so close that I almost forgot that I had a sticky-mouth secret that I mustn't tell.

'I shall do things,' I blabbed to Aunt Emma, who was nearly as mucky as me with making so many colours with little bottles and icing sugar mixed with water. 'Something you'll like even more than a million shimmer-shining stars!'

'You're sounding very mysterious, Freya.' Aunt Emma gave me one of her I-really-do-like-you smiles and I shuffled in embarrassment. People don't usually show me that they like me. They just let me tag along and help them do things.

'You've gone all shy, little traveller. What wonderful things are you going to do for me?'

Suddenly I remembered. Just in time, just before I had said even a single whisper word. My best magic had to be kept very secret or it wouldn't work. I had not even told Uncle Jack *everything*, just enough to convince him that he had to help.

I wished I'd beak-buttoned my mouth, like I was always being told to. My mam says that my mouth will be the very death of me. Hastily, I thought of the next best thing to say.

'Like making sure that baby James gets better, though I don't know why. I still think babies are messy and smelly. The daisy says that I should do my very best. The daisy says a *lot* of things.'

'Oh, I see. Witchcraft, eh?' Aunt Emma was teasing again. 'And I suppose your mam is the greatest witch of all, or does that honour belong to your great-gran?'

'Yes, she's the best choviar and the whitest, but I am a chime child. One day *I* shall be the greatest choviar. Already I'm the best dowser in all our tribe and later, when I am fully-fledge learned, I shall be the best herb lady too.'

'Oh, you're going to be a herbalist.'

'No, more of a shaman. My great-gran says a shaman has more magic, so *that* is what I shall be.'

'I'm impressed! A herbalist, a shaman and a dowser,' Aunt Emma said, quite forgetting to tell me that I was far too big for my own boots. 'Can you really discover where hidden water is? Is it very difficult to find?'

'It's open-mind easy, I learned it from the cradle. My grandad showed me that when I was not even foot-sure confident. He wanted my instinct mind to suck in the dowsing. He was stamp-foot certain that it was best for me to learn young.'

'Freya, what was the *real* reason you couldn't stay with your family, even if your mam was gone? Surely *someone* could have cared for you. You sound like a very close family indeed, to me.'

She'd asked it! She'd asked the very question that she shouldn't ask. I did the only thing I could think of . . . I fibbed . . . but I only *half* fibbed. I was getting gorgio-good at telling little white lies.

'Times is toe-tap changing. There's mostly only old ones left. My mam says that maybe I should learn out. Go to a proper school and that. She says the proper Romany days are nearly finished. All our history vardo-ashed gone! I could have stayed with my great-gran, but she can only see her hoss 'cause it's big and doesn't usually move too fast. My great-gran is really too old to care for children now and my brothers, well, they don't want to be chavi glue-stuck, do they?'

'You're very independent. It wouldn't be that much trouble, surely?'

'My mam wanted me gorgio-safe while she was gone.'

Aunt Emma smiled and nodded. That, at least, had made sense to her.

Hopping-heart hasty, I changed the subject. 'My mam says that, when Great-gran goes and they burn her wagon, our life links will be almost gone. It's a proper vardo, Aunt Emma, none of your modern rubbish. It's painted red, yellow and green. There's proper carvings in the corners. Tashar, my brother, spent hours, making sure they were all done steady-hand special. It's a vardo known to everyone. It seems wicked to have to burn it to ashes. I think Vashti, one of my bigger brothers, secretly wants to keep it too but, there again, Vashti collects *anything*.'

'Tell me more,' Aunt Emma said, pouring me a glass of orange and making herself a cup of tea.

'To me, Great-gran's vardo is like our heart centre, except it's round and shaped like a barrel. As I told you before, it's painted wide-smile bright. My great-gran loves happiness colours, just like me. It's got a big black kettle and a rack of shiny saucepans. The sort that can cook on a properly stacked log fire. There's an indoor stove too, with a chimney going up through the roof.

'We cook outside if we can. My mam says if the wind blows wrong we get too much smelly smoke inside, even in our great modern silver wagon. My mam says sheets should smell of fresh air, not of dying embers, or Dibby Gran's special stew.

'My mam made my great-gran this posh red carpet. Made it all from properly gathered wool, she did. It took ages to do. I was allowed to help with the plain bits ... It's such a pity that my great-gran's eyes are too weary white to see the fancy bits, but I can and it's wonderful posh.'

I closed my eyes. In my head, I was back home, sitting on the rich red carpet that had eaten up all our winter-time boredom. I was tracing the deep blue swirly lines with my fingers and imagining myself lost in a magic maze. It was one of my favourite things to do ... on wet days when we couldn't get out, that is.

Sometimes those curly swirls are forests and sometimes they're caves, or clouds, or secret pathways. You can be anywhere you like on that carpet. It's a far stronger magic than dancing flames.

'It took my mam years to make, Aunt Emma. She had to be real long-yawn patient and so did I. I helped sometimes, with the easy bits. Often my mam got cross, with her eyes so sore and her fingers bleeding from pulling. My great-gran was ancient-bone eighty when Mam gave it to her. She cried from happiness. She who is meddle-mole blind and can only *imagine* its loveliness!'

'Oh, Freya, that was nice of your mam, especially, when your great-gran finds it hard to see.'

'My mam says she just made it so Great-gran will be less grissle-grumpy. She says it wasn't kind at all, just practical, but none of us believed her. You'd love that wagon, Aunt Emma. There's so few left. My mam says it is a sin to burn it out. A proper sin, she says.'

'Why will they burn it? Who's *they*, Freya? Enemies?'

I knew that Aunt Emma wanted to help me to save my great-gran's wagon. I tried to explain. 'No, silly! Them's family that'll burn it to dust.'

Aunt Emma was so horrified at the very idea that she forgot to tell me off for being so rude.

'Why, Freya? Why? That's your inheritance. It must be worth a fortune.'

I nodded. 'I suppose it is. My mam says that, much as she loves our big modern caravan with its proper heating, its nice little cooker and, most of all, the tiny toilet. Much as she would hate to live in the proper wagon ... It is a bit old and

141

draughty, if I am cross-heart truthful, Aunt Emma, but that's only because it hasn't been mended properly.

'Once, it was even more cosy than the modern metal wagons with no horses. Now it *is* a bit breezy inside. Tashar would mend it more, but Great-gran won't let him. It's a time-waste to bother, she says, it will soon be burned to a cinder. All she needs at her age is happy-colour paint. Even the lovely swirly carpet that I helped my mam to make will be burned, and the heavy curtains round the chavi feather bed.'

'What's a chavi feather bed, Freya?'

I felt happier recalling the feather bed. 'When us chavis are real small, we are made to gather feathers. A chavi is a girl. We powder-clean the feathers, every one, and dry them kiss-touch carefully. Then they are stored in a big cotton sack. Collecting them, my great-gran says, becomes a lifetime habit.'

'That must take ages.'

'It does. Every downy feather we can find, we have to save.'

'What for?'

'Well, even though we collect them, nobody tongue-tells at first. It's just another job to do. That's because us chavis, like your gorgio girls, don't like boys much; though everybody says we will, when we are grown up tall. We find out pretty soon though. The older chavis delight in teasing us. "Feathers for your marriage bed," they chant. "Fancy a chavi who hates a chavo, fetching feathers for a wedding bed!" Every time they see us feather-pick, they chant. I think it's because we are brighter-eyed and often find the best.

'Lots and lots of feathers it takes, to make a bed sweet-dream soft. Great-gran gathered all her feathers herself, Mam didn't. I shall do that, Aunt Emma. I shall collect enough of my own, I will. Most Romanies don't bother now. They buy their mattresses from shops, just like you. I'm sticking to the old ways, well, as much as I can. I think that's mostly the best. I shan't be a link-chink Romany.'

I was so busy chatting that I forgot all about the pretty cakes we were supposed to be icing, and so, I think, did Aunt Emma.

'Can't your mam stop the wagon being burned?'

'Nah! But she's sad. Much as she likes our nice new home, she wouldn't want to see Great-gran's vardo burned ... not ever.'

'Surely, if she really tries, she must be able to stop the family burning it?' Aunt Emma was trying hard to imagine our little band of mostly ageing travellers, with some determined to destroy their own inheritance.

'No, you've got it wrong!'

Aunt Emma became aware that I was pulling at her skirt in my agitation. She could see my face was all screwed up in my efforts to explain. 'My great-gran says the family MUST burn the wagon. She says it's the proper thing to do. She says that, although the young moderns might steal a memento here and there, it's not right. It's not the old way.'

'But why is this so important to her?'

'Because the vardo belongs to her and everything that is hers must be gone. It must go with her to the happy place. The lovely red and yellow wagon. The pots and pans. The big kettle and pretty plates, even the beautiful swirly carpet. She wants everything burned or broken.'

'But I still don't understand why.'

'Because they are *hers* and when she goes, so must they,' I said, not quite grasping that, to a gorgio, that didn't explain anything. I picked up a cake and began my icing again.

Aunt Emma and I stood in silence for a while, each imagining the burning of the wagon when my great-gran passed on.

'We breaks one rule,' I admitted quietly after a while. 'Well, we did when my dad and grandad died.'

'What's that?' Aunt Emma asked, pretending not to notice as I gripped her legs for comfort. She, not daring to offer me a cuddle, in case I should panic and run away. Me, not liking to admit that a cuddle would suit me fine, even if it was a gorgio thing to do.

'We kept the pictures. The photos and the drawings he did by himself, especially the drawings. We keep mementoes when really, my great-gran says, we shouldn't. We don't keep the money things, just those things that are heart-treasure special to us. *That* can't be bad, can it, Aunt Emma?'

'No, I think that that's *very* nice, Freya. I'm sure that that's a perfectly proper thing to do.'

'Well, we think the photographs are family. They belong to all of us, whatever my great-gran says.

144

She only has them old brown ones herself because *her* mam hid them away when *her* mam's vardo was being ashed to nothing.'

'How does your great-gran justify keeping them?'

I laughed. 'She keeps them on the top shelf and now she's old and the old ways are even *more* important to her. She really *can't* see them . . . so she's convinced herself they could be photos of anybody.'

Aunt Emma laughed. 'Amazing, how these old folk see only what they want to see. I have an aunt who is just the same as her.'

I smiled and put down the last pretty cake that I had iced really carefully, even with all that talking, and stared unseeing at the overflowing plate.

'All them Boswell women! Everything that survives unburned is passed down through the women, Aunt Emma, even if they seem, to the gorgio eye, to be treated as unimportant. Names, traditions, photos, everything. The Romany juvel simply rule. The romnichals merely rattle.'

'You mean the men make the noise, but the women rule the roost?'

I grinned at Aunt Emma. 'You are so clever. That is exactly what I mean. All those mams and mams before them and yet almost every treasure is gone. It seems such a pity, don't you think?'

Aunt Emma dared to wrap her arms around me. They felt warm and comfy, just like my mam's would be. It was my turn to pretend. I acted as if I never noticed that warm, nice-smelling hugging. I let her hold me close, I even liked the safeness of it. I am a proper Romany and we're not supposed to be soft. I didn't cuddle back but I didn't run away.

15

'Keep your head, fulfil the drúkkerébema'

'Some says parsley must be sown nine times before it comes up.'

Uncle Jack gave me a funny look. 'It comes up the first time when I plant it.'

'Of course it does! We know these things, but it wasn't always so. Even today, parsley is still a misty-magic herb.'

Uncle Jack settled himself on the end of the bed. He sensed that I was leading up to something important. He guessed that he was going to be reminded that he had no choice but to keep his late-night promise.

'My great-gran says that her gran believed that parsley seed goes to the devil nines times and mostly forgets to come back and sprout.'

'You remember a tale like that . . . incredible.'

'No, *interesting*. Proper history through talking families.'

'Talking families.' Uncle Jack repeated my words. He says that I have strangely wise ways. Sometimes, I think, he envies me for having a much-past-time family.

'Don't you know what your greats talked

about?' I asked, knowing instinctively that he didn't. 'I suppose you were too busy being busy,' I added to excuse him.

'Freya, I can't even remember much of what my granny said. Of my great-granny, I know only that she was called Hannah and I have to confess that, before that, I don't even know a name.'

Uncle Jack looked sad, as if he had only just realised that the ancients were his family too. I gently stroked his hairy arm to show him I cared.

'But you did love your granny, I can tell.'

'Yes, but I thought her prattling was unimportant. I was too busy with exams . . . and friends.'

'Travellers might not have too many in house things, but they have a lucky life. The whole world to touch, they have, and lots of time, especially in winter. That's when our family links are most strongly forged, chatting life tales by the light of the night-time fire.'

'I have no excuse, Freya, not really. You make me feel ashamed, not even knowing my family tree. I promise you that, if ever we are lucky enough to succeed in making a baby, we'll become a proper talking family.'

I smiled, happy that he had listened so well. 'I've nearly got sandman-sleepy, Uncle Jack, but I still have something important to tell you and it's all about parsley.'

I told Uncle Jack as much as I dared about my secret plans. I needed a grown-up to help. He didn't laugh, or interrupt, even though he must have thought that I was up to something really silly. When I was sure that Uncle Jack would help as much as he could, I let myself be soothed into sleep and all too soon it was morning.

After shopping, and cleaning, Aunt Emma found me by the pond again. I loved it there. I loved slipping off my too tight shoes and swirling my feet in the cool clear water.

'I'm planning some magic ... just for you special,' I said, liking the way her face lit up when she saw me.

For a moment, Aunt Emma looked startled. Her face held her smile, but it was tinged with fear. I wished that I'd buttoned my too busy tongue. *Not enough buttons to do that! Not in all the world*, I heard my great-gran say.

Aunt Emma seemed to sense my discomfort. 'Well, mind the water,' she said lightly, changing the subject to safer things.

I laughed and offered my face to be kissed. I hadn't meant to frighten her. Earth choviars never do harm to anyone. She should've known that.

When I was sure that I was quite alone again, I dug deep into my pocket and dragged out my little felt purse. It had taken me hours to make, even with the help of my mam. I was always better at using herbs than sewing.

Inside was the smooth teardrop of quartz that had belonged to my family for ever. It was never thought to be burned or broken, not even by my great-gran. It was a secret crystal, that only the Boswell women knew of, and it was passed on from mother to daughter. Nobody ever thought to toss *that* into the pyre flames.

Normally, I wouldn't get given it until I brought

a man into our tribe and made babies of my own, but my mam was letting me care for it . . . just while she was away from me. That way I could always be sure that she was deep-love close, even if my heart felt picky panicky.

Once upon a long time ago, the crystal had had lots of shiny flat sides . . . like a diamond. I had never seen it like that and nor had any of our living family, but it had been so. My mam was insistent about that. Although it was prettier then, it was more precious now and that was because it had been worn smooth with the holding of loving fingers.

One day it would belong to me, for as long as I cared to keep it and, for me, it would do very special things.

I slowly opened my hand and gazed at our secert crystal teardrop. Having it meant that, however lonely I was, I could still be with my family. I could mind-join my thoughts with theirs. I didn't even need the powers of a chime child, not with the linking stone, and neither, as I had found out, did my mam.

I mind-joined my family at Dane's camp in Northampton. We travelled up there to meet my brother Kensa. Vashti was there too, I saw him immediately, dragging his cart of trinket treasures back to the camp to sort.

Fresh clean clothes were drying on the hedgerows. I could see them as clear as day; frocks and shawls and clean linen sheets with nice embroidered edges. All smelling fresh-air clean.

My brother Tashar was stripping for willow

pegs. Mam was feeling puffed-up proud. He was so like my dad, good with leather and brass. He made things for hosses: bridles, reins, everything.

Dad was best at catching hares and rabbits for supper. Often, he'd creep off at dusk, with the dogs and his nets and things, and almost always he came back with his huge coat pockets stuffed full.

Mostly he killed rabbits straight out, using his catapult. His dogs were Sabre and Woodpile. There were exactly trained. My brothers have never managed to get them to work as well as they did for my dad.

My dad was as sure footed as a deer. That was why we were all so very surprised when he slipped on a wet river stone. He went hunting one winter's evening and never returned. I only have little flash memories, because I was too toddle-small, but the family have painted the pictures in my mind for safe-keeping.

My brothers went out looking for my dad. Hours and hours they were gone and, when they came home, it was obvious to us all that they had been crying, even Kensa and Vashti. Romnichals are not supposed to cry.

My dad had foot-slipped on the rocks by the river while gudding fish. The water was running too high, but we were fed up with skinny rabbit. Times had been really hard that winter.

Poor Dad! He drowned, he did, even before Sabre and Woodpile could pull him back to the bank. They tried to drag him out quickly. Our dad's shirt was shredded by all those desperately pulling teeth.

That's why my mam is so fond of Tashar. He reminds her of my dad. He is her favourite and all of us know it, even though she tries not to let it shimmer-show.

My dibby gran was running round the camp, playing like the child she really is. My mam has to watch her carefully all the time. We have lots of healing things, but nothing that can make my dibby gran into a grown-up woman with a grown-up mind.

Great-gran was sitting as usual, on the steps of her vardo, enjoying the feel of the spring sun on her face, even though she can't see too much and needs telling. Everyone always spends a lot of time telling my great-gran what's happening. Sometimes they make things up . . . just so she doesn't get too bother-bored. When we run out of saying things, my great-gran fills in the spaces. My mam says that she is a rattlepot who can't bear silence . . . and whenever she says *that*, she stares at me.

Soon I would be back home with them, eating my dibby gran's special stew and playing with Fusty, Sabre and Woodpile. I would take my turn in finding an overnight field for the hoss and pony. One that was safe and full of fresh feeding grass. One where nobody would even notice that there had been an uninvited evening guest.

My mam looked up from watching Dibby. 'I'll come for you soon, Freya,' she said, her voice clear as day. 'Keep your head, fulfil the drúkkerébema just as you have been told.

'Oh yes! It's time to fulfil the drúkkerébema at

last, Freya. The family, all of the family, are waiting.'

16

'Nobody noticed at all'

From the outside Aunt Sally's house looked like a small cottage, tucked into the surrounding hillside, but inside it was truly enormous. Well, I suppose it had to be, to keep all those children real posh. Every one had a room of their own, even the new baby who wasn't nearly big enough to use it. The whole of my great-gran's vardo would have fitted into the living room . . . even the hoss!

I hid Maggie-Magpie in my carry bag, in the hope that she would be quiet, and smiled politely, like Aunt Emma said to, when we arrived. Aunt Sally gave me a wink and I ignored her. Secrets are secrets, and you are not supposed to do anything to show that you know. Not even wink.

Baby James was great-yawn boring. He lay in his frilly cot, that was far more suitable for a girl, with screwed-up eyes and fingers. I said, 'Isn't-he-lovely,' like Aunt Emma said I should do, to mind my manners, and settled down to what I thought would be a really mind-dulling afternoon.

Luckily, Maggie-Magpie was really quite tired. She'd spent hours trying to worm-catch for her-self. She'd pecked and picked at great giant worms that were far too big to chew. She was quite worn out with all that effort and sound asleep in my carry bag . . . much to Aunt Emma's relief!

A skinny girl crashed through the door as if she had every intention of smashing it down.

'Mary! How many times must I tell you to open a door before you burst through!'

'Sorry, Mum.'

Mary didn't look the least bit sorry. She spotted me and grinned. Her eyes were cornflower blue and her hair was that bright colour red that means you are bound to get a lot of teasing. Her face was full of freckles. With all that though, she was a pretty girl, real perky pretty. I liked her at once, even though she was skinnier than me, what with her being so tall.

I smiled back, my best smile, all warm and friendly. 'Hi!'

'Mary, this is Freya. She's staying with Aunt Emma for a while.'

'Hi! I suppose you've joined the endless ranks of people admiring our new baby.'

'If I tells the truth, I'm not too keen on babies,' I whispered.

'Me neither!' Mary whispered back and both of us knew that, whatever else should happen, we would always be friends.

'Can we go out, please, Mum? Can I show Freya round?'

Aunt Sally looked at Aunt Emma, who nodded. We didn't wait to see what happened next. We were wind-gust gone.

We climbed the little gully that led up by the

155

side of the half-hidden house. 'We used to have water running here once, but it's gone now,' Mary told me. 'It used to be fun having a stream running through the garden. We could grow lots of pretty primulas, drumsticks and everything. My mum would let me grow them up in the greenhouse and then, when they were ready, plant them out on the edge of the stream.'

'I like primroses to be a proper yellow, like what is natural.'

'These aren't primroses, Freya. They are just primrose-like and some of the ones that I planted didn't even resemble the wild primroses. So your precious wild flowers aren't being spoilt at all.'

I didn't want to argue, not until I knew her better. I just followed her up the gully. It was a bit of a rough climb. There were so many loose stones. I could feel Maggie-Magpie rustling in my carry bag. She was probably too busy keeping her balance to squawk.

'I'd have thought that you would like primulas,' Mary continued, as we climbed. 'You being a Romany. I was led to believe that you gypsies had a thing about bright gaudy colours.'

I pulled her towards me to see if she was wick-winding me up. If she was, I would scratch her eyes out, friend or no friend. Mary just gave me another cheeky smile. 'A little bit touchy, are we?' I recognised Aunt Emma's teasing tone and let her go.

'We are tease-taunted quite often,' I explained.

'And what do you think happens to me, with all these freckles and bright red hair? Anyone who's a little bit different gets teased. Mum says children are the cruellest things on earth and she should know, being mad enough to have seven.'

'Shall I help you get your stream back?' I asked, liking her even more.

'You can't do that! My father says the stream has been detoured somewhere upriver. He says we'll never find out where, not in a million years.'

'Your dad sounds like Uncle Jack . . . thinks he knows the answer to everything.'

We shared our first giggle. I imagined what it was like to have a sister, not a poor dead baby like Pansy, but a grown-up sister who could sneak away from gathering wood, or polishing the little cupboards in Mam's caravan, or great-gran's vardo. Someone to share secrets with . . . well, some secrets anyway.

'I've got a baby magpie in here,' I opened my carry bag, ready to let her peep in, 'and its food.'

'And pigs might fly!'

'I have! You just sit yourself down here and I'll show you.'

We settled ourselves down on the edge of the empty gully and I showed Maggie-Magpie to Mary. 'See!'

'You feed it baby food?'

'Yeah and it's growing up fine. See all those whisper-white feathers on her belly? And them there, like a shawl, above the top of her blue-black wings? She'll be able to fly off by herself soon. She can already reach the top of our great old yew . . . well, she can when she's scared anyway. I expect we'll have to say goodbye to each other, I shall be a sad-heart soon.'

I carefully fed Magpie, who watched Mary with more interest than Mary watched Magpie. 'Looks like just another baby to me. It feeds, squawks and messes down your knees. It's just like baby James, except that it's got feathers instead of a nappy.'

I had to laugh. Mary, was right.

Mary shrugged. 'If I had a baby at all, it would be a kitten. They have such huge helpless eyes and their fur is so soft. Yes, one day I might like a kitten, but not a screaming baby, or a squawking bird!'

I giggled. I *was* crazy to love such a silly bird. I just couldn't help it. I stared up the gully. 'I bet it was real pretty here, back when the water flowed,' I said, imagining frothy, tumbling white water, cascading over shining rocks.

'It *was* beautiful, Freya. I had all my own-grown plants in the garden and here on the edges of the bank. In the shade of the willows lots of your precious primroses grew. They don't grow now. It gets too hot and dry for them.'

'You find water by dowsing. I can make your water come back.'

'Dowsing? What's that?'

'You take a branch of split hazel, you know, where the branch forks like a V. You hold the ends in your hand, ever so light so they are free to move, but with just enough grip to keep the V springy. You walk along and where the water flows, even if it is devil-down deep, the hazel rods

158

twitch. Sometimes they twitch so strong that they leap right out of your hand.'

'Can I do it then?'

'Yeah! My grandad told me anyone can dowse, as long as they believe that is.'

'Believe what?'

'Why, themselves! You have to read the hazel rods, have faith in their cleverness. You have to trust in the water's pulling power.'

'Well, pulling power won't help bring the stream back, will it? After all, the water is gone. It's been gone for two years or more.'

'I'm the best dowser in our tribe. I bet I can find where the water went.'

'I bet you can't.'

'You're on!'

We slapped hands on our deal. I tucked Maggie-Magpie up safe, even though she chattered crossly. We scrambled on up towards the top of the long gully, that was also the top of the very steep hill. When we were safely there, I let Maggie sit on my shoulder for a while. She would be able to see what we were doing and she'd be a lot more comfortable.

'We need to find hazel, dogwood, or hawthorn.'

'No problem. We can find hazel in Penberry Woods over there. It won't take us long. And, anyway, the river that fed our stream is on the other side of those woods.'

'Won't your mum and Aunt Emma miss us?'

'Not for hours! You know how women are when there's babies about. My mum will let Aunt Emma nurse baby James and then they'll cluck and coo until teatime.'

There was hazel in the wood on the riverside. I scrambled up the branches and chose me a real nice fork. Not too thick and not too thin. The wood was all springy and strong, so it took me ages to bend it back and forwards until it reached its breaking time. In my head I cursed fair good, all the time I was bending it.

Back in our caravan was my really sharp knife. My mam had insisted it stayed back in the wagon. 'Gorgios think that knives are dangerous,' she'd said.

'I want to take it! How can I make things without a knife?'

'Gorgios really don't understand. We know that a Romany child is truly safe with a knife, but Emma Hemmingway will think you stupid, or dangerous. Sorry, Freya. The knife stays here!'

I wished I'd sneaked it out. My hands grew spot-red sore with bending the springy hazel. When it did break, the ends were all frayed. I had to bite off the peely bits and though they tasted nutty it was boring. The dowsing rod was OK, but I could've made a much better one using a proper knife. And I'd have done it a long time quicker.

'The next step is to follow the river.'

'I don't see the point!' Mary muttered. 'We can see that there's water here.'

'Yes, but I need to know where the water leaves the bank.'

'Oh, I can tell you that!' Mary said gleefully. 'There's an overflow pipe, just by the side of the next sluice gate. The water feeds underground to a place known as Lover's Lake.'

We followed the river and it was just as Mary said. I followed the water underground, using the twitching tingling hazel rod. Mary didn't need to show me the way. The lake was in a deep part of the woods, but all round one side it had been cleared so the sun shone through the trees and it was truly pretty.

Little seats were dotted about, so that people could sit and enjoy the water. Mary and I chose the one where our faces were made quite hot by sunshine. There was a slight breeze and birch and willow trees rustled behind us. We sat still for ages, watching the sunshine dance in the water.

Maggie-Magpie sat on the seat edge and fluffed up her feathers for a good preen in the warm sunshine. It was the first time that she had felt full-feather safe for ages.

'I envy you,' Mary said, when we were nearly fed up with watching the glittery sunshine lights reflected in the water.

'Why?'

'All that freedom! Playing all day, instead of endlessly having to help out in the house.'

'It's not like that,' I told her, putting Maggie back into the carry bag, now we were about to enter the heart of the wood.

'Caravans, tents and wagons! How long does it take to clean them? Nothing, not compared to the great white mansion I have to live in.'

'You has to be tidy in a vardo, even in our big new caravan. Compared to your posh great house, there is no room at all. My mam is like your mum. In the van things have to be just so, or she gets real crochy cross. Sometimes she yells and shouts like you just wouldn't believe.'

'But once it's clean, you're free!'

'Yeah! Free to hang out clothes on bushes. Free to wash them in a cold old stream. Free to gather firewood in the rain. And, if I'm really lucky, I might be sent out to see if there's any gorgios silly enough to want to buy lucky white heather.'

'What's a gorgio?'

'You are, silly! Anyone is, who isn't one of us.'

'Your dowsing, didn't help us to find water much, did it?'

'*Us* isn't finished yet. Now we have to find out why the water doesn't go back up your house.'

'How?'

We made our way round, through the wilder side of the lake that faced the hill running down towards Mary's house. There were little paths, all trodden out among the trees by people looking for fishing spots, but not much else. Broken branches lay rotting in the water, with leaves that had still not rotted from the winter last.

Every few feet my rods twitched, water seeped out from the lake in all directions. I had to find the bit that mattered. I had to find our bit.

'Let's walk as the crow flies towards your house.'

'Through the rough wood? Not on the trails?'

'Yes,' I said, checking that Maggie was strapped into her carry bag all safe.

We scrambled through and I kept on dowsing. Suddenly I stopped picking up water seeping and discovered the path of the old underground stream. 'It ran here?'

'How can you tell, if it's gone?'

'Well, the seeping water runs further in this direction for a start. Then I can pick up the space where the water should run, the underground tunnel that once was its home.'

'What now?'

'We go back to the lake, dowsing crossways, so I can tell whereabouts the seeping lies strongest. If we are lucky, we should find us the blockage.'

The rest was easy! My hazel dowsing rod got proper touch-twitchy at a place on the edge of the lake that was really messy. I sighed. My great-gran was right. Nothing is ever easily given.

'Do you really want that flowing water, Mary?'

'Yes, of course I do!'

'Time to get proper muddy then.'

'Mum will go mad.'

'There's no one here, just us, it being week time and spring-time breezy. Take off them clothes. We'll put them up in a tree to keep clean and dry. Then it doesn't matter if we get muddy. We can clean up after.'

'I can't take all my clothes off! Not outside!'

'Well, I can! It's straight-head sensible.'

I took off my dress and my vest and my posh flash shoes. I hung the easy-to-lose shoes carefully in a branch of the bushy willow. I hung up there too my carry bag containing Magpie. I put that where I could see it side-eye well. I needed to keep Maggie safe from hungry foxes.

'Come on! Take your clothes off, or you'll get skinned alive when you reach home.'

Mary took off her dress and her shoes and stood all knock-knee nervous, watching me.

'Oh, for goodness sake, Mary, do you want water in your precious gully or don't you?' I took off my knickers and stood as innocent as the day I was born.

Mary watched me, all wide-eyed. 'Freya, you can't go naked. It's not proper!'

'We'll see what's proper when we gets us home. Now are you going to help me, or not?'

I thought that I was going to have to do everything myself. I'd not give in now. I'd show her that I was no wimpy gorgio girl. I paddled over to one of the bigger logs and tried to shift it but, no matter how I tugged, it was far too heavy to shift. Mary watched me, still properly dressed in her white vest and flowery knickers.

'Are you going to help, or are you going to stay a great clucky chicken?'

Mary watched me guiltily. I was still straining and pulling at the great big log. 'I'll help,' she said after a long silence.

To my surprise, she waded into the water still wearing her vest and knickers. They got all soaked in an instant.

'*You'll* be half dead of cold by the time we've finished.'

'There is no way that I am taking my clothes off, Freya. People might see us!'

'What people? I can't see any and, besides, what's wrong with no clothes?'

'Freya, there are people who are bad, they could take advantage . . . my mum says that you have to be very careful. There are some people who are very bad indeed.'

'Well, they're not Romanies! We'd never hurt children, not even naked children, so they have to be gorgios. Anyway, Magpie is busy beady-eyed, so *she* will squawk out a warning.'

Nevertheless, we looked carefully round. There was not a bad person in sight. Whoever these bad people were, they did not loiter around here.

Together, we could just about move the log. It took us lots of struggling, but we did it. Then we dragged out the leaves and branches and an old dustbin liner full of rubbish and, finally, a rusty old bike and two huge tin cans.

We removed all wood and metal bits that had lain trapped behind the fallen tree. Some careless person had dumped all their rubbish there. I wished I could be sure that it wasn't one of us, but I couldn't. My brothers were often sent out to get rid of rubbish. Although *we* had never been here, I expect others of us had. Some of us were no better than gorgios where rubbish dumping was concerned.

'There, that's better!'

'How do you know? I can't see water running anywhere new.'

'No, but I can *feel* it.'

'Even without holding the dowsing rods?'

'Yes, I told you. Rods just help. They focus the mind.'

'Will the stream be running when we get back?'

'I don't suppose so,' I said, washing in a patch of clean water and drying myself with some of the dry leaves left on the ground from autumn. I scrubbed my skin hard to bring the warmth back and then climbed into my clothes. 'I expect the water will run into the ground first and then it will collect in little pockets and then it will run free, most likely after it rains.'

'I'm FROZEN!'

'Serves you right for being such a ninny!' I said unsympathetically, but then I saw that she was fair blue with cold. 'Look, take off your vest. Put on your dress when you have scrubbed warm with leaves. I promise not to look if you is shy. When you get warmer, take off them soaking wet knickers and scrub your bottom bits warm too.'

'I can't walk home with no knickers!'

'Course you can! Do you think people can see through that warm woolly dress of yours? Take off them wet clothes before you frizzle-freezes to death.'

Mary did as she was told. She was too shivery to argue. I washed out her vest and knickers in the stream as best I could and wrung them out until they were just damp, while she leaf-scrubbed herself warm.

'We're very late.'

'We'll hurry back.'

'What shall we say we've been doing? I daren't let on about the stream. Mum will go mad and, anyway, she won't believe me, not with the stream still dry.'

I picked up Magpie, still safe in her bag, even

though she had been a-peeping out, watching us and chattering to us all the time. I laughed. I was warm and happy. It had been fun, making the water go back to its proper path, really good fun, even if my arms did ache from all that log pulling. 'Don't worry! I'll pick some plants as we go back. You just agree with me. I'll have us kept proper busy.'

'That's lying, Freya!'

'No, it isn't! Not proper lying. Only white lies, like grown-ups tell all the time. Aunt Emma says that sometimes it is better to tell a white lie, than the truth which can upset someone. She said I was to say your brother James is lovely, when really I think he's quite horrid.'

'So do I!' Mary said, laughing. 'So do I.'

We held hands as we ran down the hill. Mary kept looking for water, even though I'd told her it was far too early for it to flow.

Here and there, I made us stop and pick things, special herbs, where I could. We got warmer and warmer. Our faces were quite flushed with hot by the time we got home.

'She's certainly country-wise, your Freya,' Aunt Sally said, when Mary and I returned clutching bundles of wood and field greenery. 'Look at all those different herbs and flowers!'

'What's that?' Aunt Emma asked, wanting to share Aunt Sally's enthusiasm. 'The one with the pointed leaves?'

'Skull cap. It grows on meadow banks by the river and that's groundsel and that's lady's mantle . . .'

'What are you going to do with all these?' Aunt Sally asked before I could even finish my list.

'Things!' I thought of explaining about the things I could really do, if I wanted, but Aunt Emma would only worry about my *strange little mind*, so I said, 'We're going to make flower bundles, one for you and one for Aunt Emma.'

'That's nice, dears. That's very kind.'

Aunt Emma and Aunt Sally asked me a few more questions about my collection, while Mary took the chance to slip out of the room to put on dry underwear and hide the damp stuff in the laundry basket.

'Mostly, I do nice things with plants,' I said, 'but I'm going to make a different sort of magic for the nasty man who set a trap for the dead red fox. That poor red fox had as much right to be in the field as he had. I'm going to make him very sorry that he ever set that wicked old snare. You should only set a snare if you are really really hollow-belly hungry.'

I waited, hand on hips, for the grown-ups to rise to my bait. I would obviously have to wait a very long time. Aunt Sally was used to crosspatch children. She gave Emma a wink and made a shushing gesture. 'That's nice, dear,' they chanted in unison, as if it wasn't the least bit possible, and by then Mary was safely back in the room. Nobody ever guessed that Mary came home with no knickers. It was just as I said it would be. Nobody noticed at all.

17

'She'll never do it, Freya!'

The rest of the week was quiet. I made Easter cards for Sally, Mary and baby James. I decided to make a beautifully decorated flower card for Aunt Emma and Uncle Jack. Aunt Emma had done her best to keep me amused on the days when it rained and she had introduced me to Mary and promised that we could play together often, until, that is, Mary went back to school.

She even suggested that perhaps my mam might let me stay with her in term time, so that I could go to school too. I wasn't sure what to think about that. I thought I still preferred the idea of travelling round with my mam.

I liked Aunt Emma and Uncle Jack and I had grown close too. What with Maggie and all that reading we share. Lately, he'd taken to trying to come home really early, just so he could read me long bedtime stories. He was trying to teach me to read all by myself before I went home to my mam.

Uncle Jack said that I was doing really well for starting so late. He said I was too bright for my boots, even though I haven't gotten any. He said that, if my dad was alive, he'd be really proud of me because I learn so fast. I didn't like to tell him that my dad thought that reading was all unnecessary. He thought wits were more valuable than words.

Uncle Jack used to be very quiet when I first met him. It was as if he wasn't sure about me, but when I talked of my family, he heeded real well. He even listened when I told him how I'd mixed special herbs to help make baby James better. I explained about how I'd gathered them and asked him to help me in the kitchen when Aunt Emma was out. It was part of the magic, you see. He *had* to join in too.

Also, I didn't want to scare Aunt Emma. She's not very easy-minded on the subject of spells; but I needed a chance to practise making an extra-special herbal tea. One that would put Aunt Emma in a good and happy mood. I had to make an infusion of feverwort and camomile. Uncle Jack thought I was really nice, not wanting to scare people with my white-witch ways.

I told him about my special plans for Aunt Emma. He promised not to let on. Not a single word. I wondered if he believed me. Probably he just thought he was playing a giant game of let's pretend!

Yes, I liked Uncle Jack and Aunt Emma. I would definitely do them some magic. However, I worried me. Making the magic was *not* going to be easy, even with a little help from Uncle Jack.

When Mary and I had our stream-water adventure. When we had to get ourselves undressed. Well, at least, I did, so as we could pull out that great big log. Then I understood how very hard it was going to be, that it would be almost impossible to get Aunt Emma to do the magic properly. The special magic that would make her and Uncle Jack very happy indeed one day.

'She *never* do it, Freya! She'll NEVER EVER do it!' Uncle Jack warned me when I told him what he had to help me make her do.

'She *has* to, Uncle Jack! We have only one chance. I didn't intend to tell you, well, not that bit, but after Mary was so shy, and she still a child, I knew I couldn't do the magic all by myself. Not even if I give her my special herbal tea to drink before it gets starting.'

'Freya, darling, I am overwhelmed by your trust . . . quite quite overwhelmed and I promise not to breathe a word to anybody, especially not Em, but I really think she'll never do it . . . not in a month of Sundays.'

He had to be wrong! HE HAD TO BE WRONG!

'My mam says if you wants something badly enough, it will happen!' I told Uncle Jack stuffily. 'So you really do have to help me out!'

'I'll try, Freya, I promise I'll try and that's really all I can do.'

I knew that, for the moment, I must be satisfied. I went back to my cards. I made a really nice Easter card for my mam. Aunt Emma found me an envelope that was just the right size. 'She'll be back soon, I expect,' I said to the unasked question in her mind.

The following day there were things to buy

again. If I hadn't nagged for hours about how I longed to play with Mary, I think we'd've been shopping all day for lots more of those posh foods in pretty packages, with no taste at all. A waste of time, my mam says, and she is right, I'm sure that she is, so I nagged and nagged about how I wanted to go and play with my new-found friend.

I was desperate to visit Mary again, especially after I'd earwigged a very interesting telephone talk. I hadn't meant to, but when I heard Aunt Emma say, 'Oh-that-must-be-nice,' followed by, 'I-bet-Mary-will-grow-her-primulas-again,' well, then I knew that the gully was running once more with sweet fresh water.

After I'd pestered her silly, Aunt Emma finally decided. 'It would be rather nice to chat to Sally again,' she said, 'and I do have a present for the new baby.' So off we went. That meant Aunt Emma, Maggie and I could see the new stream for ourselves and, if I was lucky, Mary, Maggie and me would have time for a proper indoor play.

This time I wasn't going to spend all day beavering about in a cold spring lake. I was really glad that I'd done the job properly the first time round.

'What shall us do?' I asked as soon as we had gone through all the politeness that Aunt Emma and Aunt Sally considered proper and admired the nicely flowing water from every single angle.

'Mum says we bigger girls can have the play room to ourselves. That's you, me, Elizabeth and Antonia.'

I felt nervous. I could cope with one gorgio girl but three all at once? Suddenly, I felt out of my

172

depth. I didn't know much about gorgio chavis and how they played.

Mary nearly guessed what I was thinking in my head. 'If I said me and Tony and Lizzie, would that sound better?'

'We've got posh names too. We has Elizabeths and Carolines and Lurendas.'

'Lurenda!' Antonia said, her eyes wide open in excitement. 'Well, that's got to be the name of a princess. I think we should open up the clothes box.'

I looked at the missy Antonia Reed. She was only just younger than me, but I felt much more grown up than her, even more grown up than Mary who was two years older.

'A clothes box for games?' I'd imagined us doing things, not strutting round wearing fancy clothes. Fancy clothes were for festas and weddings, not playing.

'Come on, Freya!' Mary called, as she raced upstairs. 'You'll have fun. You wait and see.' Maggie just sat there. I think that, at that moment, she felt as mousy-minded as me.

I followed the girls upstairs and hung Maggie's carry bag on to the back of a door hook, so that she could see.

The play room was huge! It ran all across the top of the house. Where everything else seemed to be painted plain white, or soft pastel colours, the playroom walls were different. Each wall had things painted over it. Country scenes, rabbits and elephants. Flowers and birds. It was wide-eyed wonderful!

'Who did that?' I asked. 'Who painted all them things?'

'Our dad. He's a graphic artist.'

'What's that?'

'I don't really know. He draws things for people and, when we ask him nicely, he draws things for us. Come and look over here. See. Princesses and wizards and fairies. Everything.'

It was magic! All the things drawn in vibrant colour. Toadstools with little elves, yellow primroses just like they should be, resting in the seeding grass, all properly life-like. There were even dragonflies and ladybirds and the lush green grasses that live in a meadow, waving seed heads and everything.

'I never knew *anyone* who could paint like that!'

'Well, if you really want me to, I'll ask Dad to show you sometime.'

I nodded. I would play let's pretend or anything, so that I could be shown how to paint, just a little bit, like that.

Little Lizzie opened the clothes box. I had expected things to be all neatly folded, like they were in our wagon. Everything in its place, so that we were left with space to get in ourselves.

The clothes box, however, was not like that at all. It was heaped with brightly coloured things. There were dresses and shawls and shoes with heels so high that you could barely walk. I knew, even before I tried them on, that they would hurt my feet something wicked. There would be black blisters promised, if I even wore them for more than a moment. I didn't care! They were so pretty.

I took off my flash new shoes and tried them for size. They were either too big, or too small, but I didn't care. There were pink shoes with point tips and pearls, square white shoes with neat little bows, different-coloured leathers, lots of kinds of patterns . . . everything. I chose myself a pale blue pair of shoes with the highest heels you could imagine. After all, they had promised that I was going to be a princess. Lizzie laughed at me as I struggled to walk.

'Well, you'll have to practise more, to look as proud as a princess.'

'And she'll need a posh frock.'

I rummaged through the box with Mary and Lizzie. We tipped everything out on the floor to make sure that nothing was missed.

'She should wear the wedding dress that Granny Lester gave us.'

'Yes, she should.'

I let Mary help me into the lacy white wedding dress, that was only a bit moth-eaten. There were lots of beautiful pearl buttons all down the back. It took Mary ages to do them all up. I admired myself in the mirror. I felt like a princess. While the others were dressing up, I borrowed a comb and tried to make my wild black hair look princess tidy.

Mary decided to be the prince, as she was tallest. She put on some black trousers and tied a brightly coloured scarf round her waist for a belt. She found a patterned shirt and a bright red waistcoat and put them on too. Last of all, she popped on her head a big felt cap. I thought she looked a bit like Kokko George, but I didn't say so. If she'd worn a big earring, or a handkerchief, she would have been spitting-image similar.

'We need jewellery.'

'And make-up.'

Yet more boxes were opened. The playroom was a wonderful place. It had everything . . . except the bright red lipstick that I really needed to be a princess. I was about to be disappointed for the very first time, when Lizzie gave me an impish grin and slipped away. She came back with a lipstick that was deep as warm ripe peaches. 'That will do fine,' I said, ignoring the fact that she had probably borrowed it from her mother and most likely taken it with not asking.

Antonia had chosen to be the most evil wizard in the whole wide world. She dressed herself all in black. She even found a black shawl to use as a cloak. Mary said all wizards had to wear them and they have to have a wand, so their spells would work properly. The wand turned out to be a stick, covered with silver paper, that they had used before.

We decided that Maggie-Magpie could join in too. By now, she was making a lot of noise and wasn't the least scared. I think she liked being in the company of so many chatty children.

'Your Magpie can be a crow!' Lizzie suggested. 'Wizards often have cats or crows like witches.'

'I thought it was ravens,' Mary said.

I shrugged. 'Don't know! Maggie can be whatever it is. Maggie can be the wizard's evil servant to equal Lizzie, who's my good one.' I put Maggie gently on to Antonia's shoulder and, to my surprise, she stayed there, just like she did on mine.

That settled, we decided to make Antonia a pointed wizard's hat. We were lucky, there was one on the wall to copy. The wall wizard didn't have an animal at all, just a big cauldron for mixing spells, so our wizard would be even better.

Out came the crayons and paper, scissors and glue. The hat had to be cut and folded just right. Mary showed us how. We made big silver and gold stars for it. It took ages to get them exactly star-shaped! I made the biggest one all by myself! Now I knew why let's pretend was such fun. I felt like I could play it for ever and ever!

'ARE YOU GIRLS COMING DOWN FOR TEA?'

We looked at each other. We hadn't *even started* to play.

'CAN WE HAVE OURS UP HERE, PLEASE?'

The answer was yes. So now we had another game. The prince had to rescue me from the wicked wizard and his evil magpie, very quickly so as we could eat. Lizzie had to help the prince because she was my servant. Then the wizard had to promise that he would be good for ever and ever, so that we could invite him for tea.

All this took far longer than we had planned.

I had to struggle to resist the wizard's evil spells. Lizzie had to do a lot of screaming so as to protect me. I was a princess, so I had to look scornful and proud, knowing that my prince would rescue me and my trusty servant in the end. Only then could we live happy ever after, like Mary said we should.

None of us even saw who brought up the tea. We were too locked up in playroom magic. Besides, if we didn't watch the wizard, then he'd turn us into frogs, using the wand and Magpie. So it was important to out-magic him first.

We had neat little sandwiches on a china plate, just right for a princess. We had a big chocolate cake to share between us and rabbit-shaped biscuits with fresh orange to drink.

I grabbed the orange and so Lizzie reminded me that I was a princess and had to hold out my little finger like a lady does. I looked at her all blank like and so she showed me. 'It's easier with a cup and saucer, but you don't drink orange from a cup and saucer, so you'll have to pretend.'

I didn't mind. I was getting quite good at pretending.

'What's your favourite food?' Mary asked when we'd become more interested in chocolate cake than castles.

'Hotchi-witchi.'

'What's that?'

'Hedgehog.'

'HEDGEHOG!' Three pairs of eyes turned all their attention to me. 'HEDGEHOG!'

'Hotchi-witchi is delicious. You catch your hedgehog and he does what hedgehogs always do.'

'What's that?' Lizzie asked, her chocolate cake quite forgotten.

'Curls up in a ball,' Antonia told her crossly. 'Everyone knows that.'

'And then?'

'Then you have to uncurl him. You tickle his back with a fine stick and he unfolds.'

Three pairs of eyes stared at me with horror. I grinned and continued. 'Then you hit him on the nose. One little tap an' he's stone-cold dead.'

'That's cruel!'

'No crueller than electrocuting a cow, or wringing a chicken's neck!' Mary said, coming to my defence. 'And probably kinder, because the hedgehog doesn't have to travel in a lorry, or queue to be killed, does it?'

'I shall *never* eat meat again,' Antonia whispered.

I stared at her scornfully. 'Do you think them cows will be in the field if you don't eat them. Or those sheep and fluffy lambs? Do you think your farmers will keep them there just to look pretty? Well, do you?'

Lizzie looked doubtful. Antonia was still rigid with indignation.

'No, of course they won't,' I snapped, 'and don't forget that pretty wood of yours. If your rich gentry couldn't shoot, do you think that it would stay a wood, just for your enjoyment? Do you think all those wild things would be there? NO! It would be turned into yet another rape field, or something that makes better money mountains. At least we kill to eat, not like your game gentry, simply for pleasure.'

'How do you cook hedgehog?' Mary asked, wanting to return our thinks to safer things.

'The best way is baking in clay. That keeps in

all the flavour. We add a bit of agrimony and a bit of sorrel.'

'What's that?'

'Herbs,' Mary said. 'Freya showed me them the other day.'

'Anyway, hotchi-witchi is much better than your chickens, that never even see the light of day.'

'I shall *never* eat meat again,' Antonia said, her face fluffy-flour white. 'Not *any* meat.'

'So what will you wear on your feet? And is a posh madam like you never going to have anything but a horrid plastic handbag?'

Antonia couldn't answer. I guessed she really hated the idea of plastic shoes and handbags. I understood why. There is something really wonderful about the smell of well-cured leather. She fled downstairs and, because she did, Lizzie followed.

I looked at Mary, with tears struggling to escape from my eyes. 'I didn't mean to upset them. I just wanted to try and explain how we think and *why* we do. I wanted her to feel for our Romany ways.'

Mary took my hand, to show me we were still friends. 'They'll soon forget. It's a matter of custom. We don't eat hares or hedgehogs, you don't hunt for fun. It's not better, or worse, Freya. It's just different.'

We gave each other a hug before following the other girls downstairs. Mary was right. We were soon friends once more but, as far as I know, Antonia never again ate meat.

18

'Things were going very badly indeed'

Good Friday morning dawned fair and warm. Aunt Emma woke early but I was up before her, bustling round in the kitchen, trying, and failing, to be quiet. It was important to get everything just right . . . ever so important indeed.

I heard Aunt Emma nudge Uncle Jack. 'Freya's up to something! Those are very important bustling noises, even for a Good Friday surprise.'

I shivered with nervousness. Aunt Emma was going to get a surprise all right. I hoped that Uncle Jack would help me, like he promised.

'Freya's making us tea, silly,' I heard him say. 'Now lie down and pretend to be asleep when she comes in. She's trying to make the day special for us, after all.'

The day was going to be special all right . . . very special. Aunt Emma wouldn't guess *how special* for ages.

After a lot of effort I was ready. I carried up breakfast tea on the posh silver tray that I had spent ages elbow-grease polishing the day before so that it really shone, just as Aunt Emma liked.

I put a clean, neatly pressed napkin on the silver

tray, with my extraordinary herbal tea. Lastly I added a vase full of freshly picked wild flowers. The tray looked beautiful, but it was ever so difficult to carry. I had to walk very carefully indeed. It took ages to bring it all the way upstairs without spilling a single drop.

'Good morning, Aunt Emma. Good morning, Uncle Jack,' I said politely, minding my best manners so as to please them.

'Good morning, Freya. This is most kind,' Aunt Emma said, rewarding me with one of her brightest smiles, even though the cock had not long crowed and first church hadn't even thought of starting.

I sat patiently on the edge of the bed, while they drank my herbal tea. My great-gran had taught me the recipe, almost as soon as I was big enough to make hot tea and that was ages ago. It was a tonic tea, one designed to make people feel happier.

I could tell that Aunt Emma thought the tea tasted a teeny bit odd. It was written all over her face, even though she was too polite to say so. She was more used to shop-packaged tea.

I was determined she would drink every drop. This was supposed to be a very magical day, she should start it off just right. Aunt Emma just had to be put in the mood to please.

Luckily, no matter what she really thought in her head, Aunt Emma said that I'd made the tea just right. When they had finished every drop, I decided that they were ready to listen to my favour.

'Aunt Emma, will you do something *important* for me?' I said, saying my words slowly and carefully, so that she would be impressed. 'Will you help me plant some parsley seeds? They're special parsley seeds and they have to be planted at exactly the right time and the time is nearly now.'

'Why?' Aunt Emma asked, putting down her cup. 'Parsley's not that special. It's only a herb.'

'It is! It's a special herb, everybody should plant some.' My voice was pleading. Aunt Emma had to realise that she *must* help me.

Aunt Emma sat up in the large flowery bed, that didn't hold a single real feather, and gave me one of her patient smiles.

'You don't have to plant parsley seeds, Freya. The vicar has oodles of parsley plants. I'm sure that he can spare you some, if you ask him nicely.'

Things were not going to plan. Aunt Emma wasn't too keen on food gardening. I was well aware of that. I turned to Uncle Jack for help. 'Giving parsley roots away gives bad luck too. Everyone knows that, don't they, Uncle Jack?'

Aunt Emma looked at her man, as if waiting for him to shake his head. He didn't. He nodded. 'Parsley has to be planted in the right manner to bring good luck. My father was one of the best gardeners in the world and he *never* parted willingly with his parsley.' He gave me a sly wink when Aunt Emma couldn't see. 'It's *very* unlucky to give parsley roots away. Perhaps she could *steal* some?'

'Jack, don't be so silly. Of course she can't steal some. If it's really that important, then tomorrow we'll go and buy some seeds.'

'Tomorrow's no good!' I was struggling not to shout. 'I have some seeds anyway. Uncle Jack bought them for me last week because I asked him to . . . very nicely.'

'That was kind of you, darling,' Emma said to Uncle Jack, and then she turned towards me. 'So why, if they are so important, didn't you plant them when Uncle Jack was nice enough to go out and fetch them for you?'

I grinned. She wouldn't think he was so nice when she knew what was to follow. Indeed she wouldn't.

'The parsley seeds *have* to be planted today, that's why.' I cuddled up close to her, just as she liked me to. My mam never did that. She says that too much cuddling makes for great big softies. I tried again.

'My mam says it's important to plant parsley on Good Friday and so does my great-gran.'

'Well, there's plenty of time yet. The day has barely started.'

'Yes, but you have to sow it when the church bells are ringing,' I hurried through my sentence, hoping she wouldn't notice the next bit too much, 'and you have to plant it with no clothes on.'

She noticed!

Aunt Emma sat bolt upright in bed and her face went bright scarlet at the very idea. 'Freya, you're *joking*? You really must be joking!'

Uncle Jack sniggered, desperately trying to cover his face with his hands as if he was scratching his nose. 'She's serious, darling! Now be a nice little foster-mother and go and help plant the lucky parsley seeds.'

'If you think that I am going to plant parsley

seeds, sweet mother-naked, then you must be out
of your tiny mind!'

Aunt Emma was fighting up all indignant now
and even I was having a job not to laugh. She
looked hot-smoking embarrassed. Even the idea
had turned her face to purple.

Uncle Jack sniggered again and hurriedly pretended to sneeze. Aunt Emma still sat pole-rigid in
bed, shaking her head as if in disbelief.

I stared at them both with undisguised disap-
pointment. They were laughing at me. Large tears
welled up in my eyes. Gypsy tears that should
never be shed, not even at funerals. I was properly
upset. After all, I only wanted to show them how
much I cared. I only wanted to give them a loving
gift in return for their kindness. I only had a
drúkkerébema to fulfil.

'My mam *says* . . .' I pleaded desperately, with
real tears streaming down my face.

'Your mam can say whatever she likes! There is
NO WAY that I am going to stand mother-naked
in my very own garden and plant stupid parsley
seeds while church bells chime!'

I was lost for words. *Me*! Things were going
very badly indeed.

'*Oh, go on, Em*! You can see what it means to
the child.' Uncle Jack had stopped laughing and
was trying to fix a concerned expression on to his
face. 'Freya's obviously missing her mum at Easter.
You *know* how important these strange traditions
are to a Romany child and, if not, you should do.'

He leaned over and turned her face to his. 'The
garden's secluded enough, for goodness sake, Em.

Nobody will see you, I'm sure. Go and plant the seeds, just for Freya. It won't take a moment after all. Go on, *I dare you*!'

'It's no good playing dare with me!' Aunt Emma told Uncle Jack crossly. 'This is Good Friday, *not* April the first.'

'Oh, go on, Em! The child needs a home-comfort ritual at Easter, not having her mum and all that. Go and plant a few silly seeds, for goodness sake.'

'*Not* mother-naked!' Aunt Emma's face was now as white as her fresh clean sheets.

'It's no good looking at me all cow-eyed! I won't!' she hissed at me.

I almost gave up. I remembered how Mary had refused to take off her vest and knickers, insisting on getting wet and cold, rather than be for a moment as nature made her.

Uncle Jack saw that I was losing heart for my magic. He tried again.

'Oh, go on, Emma! Do it exactly as Freya says. Do it just to please her . . . and me.' He gave Aunt Emma a hug and kissed her gently, right on the lips.

'Come on, super foster-mum. You once told me you'd do *anything* for a child and here's one plead-ing. Who's to know except us? And I promise not to tell a soul. Not even the milkman.'

I stood before them, with tears still running down my face. Salty tears that streak-line stung. I tried to wipe some away as Uncle Jack spoke. I could see the funny side of things, really I could, even while I was so busy crying.

It was not as if I was even sure that I wanted to

be in the garden with a mother-naked Aunt Emma. I would be embarrassed too, her being all gorgio-grown, but it was *necessary*. I had succeeded in making my face black and smudged with miserable tears. 'Please!' I pleaded one last time. 'It's so *important*!'

Aunt Emma's face flashed from mine to Uncle Jack's and back again and then, just when I thought that I really couldn't stand the tension between us any more, her shoulders slumped in quiet resignation.

The church bells began to ring. Urgently I drag-ged the reluctant Aunt Emma from her nice warm bed. Uncle Jack walked beside us wearing his let's-humour-this-changeling-child expression.

Maggie-Magpie flew unbidden from my room as we passed. She landed on my shoulder. I remem-bered the play room . . . and felt like a wizard. Only instead of a raven, a hat and a wand I had a magpie and a little packet of seeds.

I led them to a little bare patch of earth at the side of the vegetable garden. I gave Aunt Emma a stick to make nice little drills and I pointed to a small pile of fine tilth earth that I had put all ready, so that she could cover them up, once planted.

Aunt Emma clutched her dressing-gown to her thin body, obviously feeling incredibly stupid. She stood, my little seeds tight in her folded hand. I think she was still determined to plant them with-out removing a stitch of her clothing.

Uncle Jack waved his arms about. 'See, I told you! There's not a soul about. Get mother-naked,

Emma! Do just as poor little gypsy Freya says. Quickly now, or the truly keen will begin to arrive for early morning church.'

Aunt Emma looked at Jack and me, registering our determined faces. She wore a my-God-what-can-I-do expression.

We stood still wearing our best hurry-up looks. Time seemed to stop in that lightly frost-dressed garden.

After what seemed like for ever, Aunt Emma gave in. She removed her housecoat as fast as she could and, shivering with cold, she planted the seeds in a furious flurry of naked activity.

I could tell Aunt Emma was frightened that we would laugh and waken the neighbours. She was praying that they hadn't all taken it into their heads to go to early morning church. The planting took seconds. To poor frightened Aunt Emma, sowing a few little seeds must have seemed to take endless hours.

She did it so fast that I was scared they weren't planted properly, but when I checked, they were. Aunt Emma had obviously no intention of planting the seeds twice, even if they were very special indeed.

Just as she was nearly finished, Maggie heard something and squawked out a warning.

'Oh no! Not the Plumptons,' squealed Aunt Emma.

Uncle Jack was already holding out Aunt Emma's housecoat. She scrambled back into it, as fast as she could. I was amazed at the speed that she moved. Thin arms shot into droopy sleeves.

The tie belt was flung wide and, in no time at all, the only sign you could see that Aunt Emma had ever been mother-naked was a pair of very shaky legs.

Maggie was silent now. The rustling had been unimportant really, just the sound of a mousing cat. Only Maggie had bad memories of cats, even if she was sitting safely on my shoulder.

I rushed up to Aunt Emma, now she was decently covered again, and plastered her face with the kisses that gorgios like so much.

'Thank you, Aunt Emma. Thank you so much! You did it exactly right. You planted the parsley just as my mam and my great-gran said you should.'

'But why? Why did I have to do such an awful thing?' Aunt Emma was fair shaking with worry. 'You won't tell that social worker, will you? She'll think you're an abused child and she'll never let me care for a lonely child again.'

I felt her fear, the same fear that had made her plant seeds, naked as the day she was born. The fear of losing the love of a child like me.

'I'll never tell *anyone*,' I promised, liking her better than I ever had before. 'I promise to tell nobody except my mam and my great-gran.'

'Do they really *have* to know?'

I nodded. 'Only my mam and my great-gran. I promise millions.' They *have* to know . . . after all, it is my very first special magic.

Maggie-Magpie gave me her most chattery squawk. I stroked her head and met her beady eye. 'OK, so you helped,' I admitted, 'but only a *bit*.'

19

'To Aunt Emma and Uncle Jack, with love from Freya'

Aunt Emma felt sad. I could see it in her face. It was Aunt Emma who was hiding the tears this time, not me.

I was about to disappear, just as suddenly as I had arrived. Aunt Emma knew that was the problem with short-term fostering, but it didn't stop her crying. Her big house would seem far too quiet and far too empty again.

I stood, the red carry bag containing Maggie over my shoulder, clutching my mam's hand and a bag full of lets-go-shopping clothes. Aunt Emma and Uncle Jack looked pouty-faced sad. I promised that I'd visit them soon.

'How soon?'

'As soon as my mam and Maggie and me comes this way.'

'We could always care for Freya, Mrs Boswell, if you decided that it was time for her to go to a proper school. We would be more than pleased to look after her.'

My mam said nothing. Aunt Emma looked as if

she was about to cry some more. Even Uncle Jack was a little red-eyed.

My mam shuffled, she was impatient to get away. 'I'll think on it, missus,' she said at last.

'You really will let her come and visit us?' Aunt Emma pleaded desperately. 'You can even bring Magpie!' she said, looking hopefully at me.

'I'll come quite soon,' I promised, giving them both another hug and kiss, 'even if Maggie isn't allowed in the dining room, or the kitchen.' We all giggled nervously and I hugged them again.

My mam looked at me all startled and then she smiled and nodded in agreement. 'Yeah, I'll let hers visit you soon, if she likes yer both so much.'

In my mind, as we travelled back to our camp, I could see Aunt Emma as she wandered round her neat tidy rooms, not knowing what to do with herself. Then I pictured her in her bedroom, dreamy-eyed, staring at the hazelnut potpourri I had made for her as a leaving present. She would be tracing her fingers over the fading flowers, mixed in with parsley and sage, just like she did when she passed a beautiful ornament, or a rose in the garden.

I wondered how long it would be before she noticed that I'd left them my favourite teddy bear. The only toy I owned that was package shop-made. My dibby gran had rescued it from a tip, still in a battered box, but she had soon become bored with it and gave it to me when I was tiny. My mam scrubbed it clean and gave it new eyes and I loved it to bits.

I left it by the side of the bed, the side where

she slept and I used to sit, when we all snuggled up for a cuddle in the mornings. I left my teddy, not by accident, but with a big label round his neck saying: 'To Aunt Emma and Uncle Jack, with love from Freya.'

The words were spelled out with loving care. Just as Uncle Jack had taught me. There was not one single bit of wrong.

I knew that, when Aunt Emma saw my teddy, her eyes would fill with tears, but her tears would be more happy than sad because I had shown that a little bit of me was sad to go home. She would understand that I had left her a small memento, something that would make her missing me seem just a little bit easier.

'Freya, you're a special child,' she had whispered every night that I was with them. 'We'll miss you something terrible when you go home to your mam.'

I am free again. My hair blows wild in the wind. I can take off my pink flash shoes and help my mam in the miles of magic woods and fields that are like a garden to us. Maggie comes with me everywhere. She is well grown up now and should be finding a friend so as to bring us some fun . . . you know!

> *One for sorrow*
> *Two for mirth*
> *Three for a wedding*
> *Four for a death . . .*

I thought everyone knew that!
Maggie-Magpie stays close by my side. Even

though she could make good use of her lovely shiny wings. Whenever she chooses, she is free to go. She comes with me everywhere and I think that that is the most wonderful thing of all. No matter what my great-gran mutters as she scowls at Magpie from the front of her vardo.

Emma Hemmingway seems to me a million miles away. I feel surprised that I miss her and Uncle Jack as much as I do. I wonder if I should ask my mam if I could try a gorgio school. I wonder if their life is as good as mine. I don't think so.

Two months have passed since I came home. Passed all in a flash they have. Last night I dreamed a special telling dream. I saw the moment when Aunt Emma would run to Sally with her news:

'I'm *pregnant*, Sally. You won't believe it, but I really am! After *all* these years of failure.'

'Wonderful! And you thought it was impossible too.'

Aunt Sally wouldn't be the least bit surprised. Of course she wouldn't, but she'd never let on. Not in a million years.

My dear friend Mary stood clear in my mind. She was there, behind Aunt Sally, clutching a tiny wide-eyed baby of her own. A little pink-tongued kitten that Aunt Emma failed to notice, so great was her excitement.

'Jack says that my being pregnant has everything to do with Freya and nothing at all to do with doctors.'

'Freya?' Oh, how innocent Aunt Sally would sound.

In my mind I could see her clutching a much

193

bigger and healthier Jamie to her chest and trying desperately hard not to laugh, because she had known all along how I came to be there.

'Remember me telling you that Freya made me plant parsley seeds, mother-naked on Good Friday?' Aunt Emma would continue, blushing even at just the remembering.

I smiled in my head. I could see her standing like a shy gorgio schoolgirl, as she told Aunt Sally her news. Her hands protectively folded over her newly growing tummy.

'She *insisted* that the parsley had to be planted when the church bells rang. Jack thought it was so funny, me planting seeds in the nude, but I just wanted to *die*!'

'Well, yes! I'm not liable to forget that little tale, am I?' Sally would say, feeling safe now to laugh out loud.

'And Jack even agreed to help her, just because she told him that when the parsley germinated I would become pregnant, *and, isn't it silly! I have!*'

'Fancy Jack playing along!' Aunt Sally would tease.

'He just wanted to please her, he likes kids,' Aunt Emma would excuse him, her voice bubbling over in excitement. 'Freya told him something else too. She said the baby would be a girl and that, eventually, she would marry James. I don't think he actually *believed* it but, after all this, who's going to lay odds on that?'

Aunt Sally would smile and keep her family secrets. She who had a mam, who was married to a man, whose dad was a long-since-gone Romany.

She in her posh house, pretending that she had never, ever, made the special arrangements that meant my mam moving away and me sharing the Hemmingway home for Easter.

It was her chattering to my mam, who was selling her a basket, soon after the visit from Kokko George, that started me on the way to my very first big healing magic. Aunt Sally, having six kids, and another on the way, and her best friend Emma not even having one. Later, Kokko George used a similar basket to carry my purring memento present back to Mary.

'We can help,' my mam had promised that day. 'Great-gran is *always* willing to do a little something for her family, even if they are of poshrat origin.' Aunt Sally had needed to say no more.

I *still* miss Aunt Emma and Uncle Jack. They were kind to me when I did my first magic. When I was still so young that I missed my mam. The baby is nearly two months old now. She's pretty and kind, just like her mum. I think I might visit again. I think Aunt Emma should have another baby, only this time a boy child for Uncle Jack. I don't like babies me, not really, but my mam says that when I am quite grown up, I will most likely change my mind.

Romany Words Used

Athinganoi	a particular tribal caste
Buni Manridi	honey cake
Chavi(s)	girl(s)
Chavo	boy
Chíriko	bird
Chokkas	boots
Choviar	witch
Didakai	half-Romany
Drúkkerébema	prophecy
Festas	celebrations
Gorgio	non-gypsy
Hotchi-witchi	hedgehog
Juvel	Romany women
Kackaratchi	magpie
Kokko	uncle
Koshti Bok	good luck
Kushti	good, fine
Motto	drunk
Mumper(s)	non-gypsy traveller(s), tramp(s)
Patteran	road sign
Poshrat	half-blood
Prala	brother
Romnichals	Romany men

Rokker	talk
Sastra Pot	stew
Shoshi	rabbit
Vardo	gypsy wagon

A Little Gypsy History

Gypsies are a nomadic people. Their origins have become a little lost in the mists of time. It is almost certain that the gypsy originated in India. They were most likely to have been a tent-dwelling people of fairly low caste.

The word gypsy is actually a corruption of the word Egyptian, and one theory was that the gypsy may have originated in Little Egypt, which in itself is confusing, as this has been variously considered to be Egypt, Little Armenia and Epirus.

Gypsies are known as Arzigans or Athinganoi in Asia Minor. These names are derived from an Indian sub-caste, with the meaning 'not to be touched'. Many of them were said to earn their living by sorcery.

Romanes is predominantly a spoken language, passed from mouth to mouth, in a travelling culture. The backbone of the Romany language is Indian, corrupted, or adapted over the passage of time, with additions from countries such as Iran (Persia), Romania, Turkey, Hungary and, eventually, Western Europe.

For a people so widely travelled, it is surprising

how constant the Romanes language is, despite regional variations. This is probably due more to dialect than evolution. The pure Romany gypsies that I have spoken to are extremely proud of still having a language that can be understood, no matter where they travel.

True Romanies remain a proud race, with a very individual culture, which, even if not strictly adhered to today, is of great historic importance. Their greatest fear seems to be the intrusion into their lifestyle caused by the modern Traveller.

Romany gypsies, have always considered themselves, to be a race apart. I believe that they should be allowed to remain so. It would be a great loss to society if a culture that has existed so successfully, for so long, should be destroyed.

Gold and Silver Water

Elizabeth Arnold

Freya is summoned to help Penny, a girl
lost in sadness. But even Freya's
Romany magic cannot seem to unlock
Penny's tightly imprisoned feelings.

In a race against time, Freya is left with
one final option. She must discover the
power of gold and silver water. Only
then will Penny be healed. Only then
can Freya return home where she longs
to be.

Highly commended by the TES NASEN
Special Education Needs Award

A Riot of Red Ribbon

Elizabeth Arnold

Freya faces her greatest challenge yet. Little Briar Rose and Dibby Gran have disappeared and only Freya, with her Romany magic and the ancient linking crystal, can find them.

Freya and her best friend Mary set out following the lost pair on horseback. But can their friendship stand the test when both girls fall for the enchanting Churen Isaacs?